THE KICKLEBURYS
ON THE RHINE.

William Thackeray Makepeace

Copyright Notice

Any reader who may have a fancy to purchase a copy of this present edition of the "History of the Kickleburys Abroad," had best be warned in time, that the Times newspaper does not approve of the work, and has but a bad opinion both of the author and his readers. Nothing can be fairer than this statement: if you happen to take up the poor little volume at a railroad station, and read this sentence, lay the book down, and buy something else. You are warned. What more can the author say? If after this you WILL buy, – amen! pay your money, take your book, and fall to. Between ourselves, honest reader, it is no very strong potation which the present purveyor offers to you. It will not trouble your head much in the drinking. It was intended for that sort of negus which is offered at Christmas parties and of which ladies and children may partake with refreshment and cheerfulness. Last year I tried a brew which was old, bitter, and strong; and scarce any one would drink it. This year we send round a milder tap, and it is liked by customers: though the critics (who like strong ale, the rogues!) turn up their noses. In heaven's name, Mr. Smith, serve round the liquor to the gentle-folks. Pray, dear madam, another glass; it is Christmas time, it will do you no harm. It is not intended to keep long, this sort of drink. (Come, froth up, Mr. Publisher, and pass quickly round!) And as for the professional gentlemen, we must get a stronger sort for THEM some day.

The Times' gentleman (a very difficult gent to please) is the loudest and noisiest of all, and has made more hideous faces over the refreshment offered to him than any other critic. There is no use shirking this statement! when a man has been abused in the Times, he can't hide it, any more than he could hide the knowledge of his having been committed to prison by Mr. Henry, or publicly caned in Pall Mall. You see it in your friends' eyes when they meet you. They know it. They have chuckled over it to a man. They whisper about it at the club, and look over the paper at you. My next-door neighbor came to see me this morning, and I saw by his face that he had the whole story pat. "Hem!" says he, "well, I HAVE heard of it; and the fact is, they were talking about you at dinner last night, and mentioning that the Times had – ahem! –'walked into you. –”

“My good M–” I say – and M– will corroborate, if need be, the statement I make here – “here is the Times' article, dated January 4th, which states so and so, and here is a letter from the publisher, likewise dated January 4th, and which says:–

“MY DEAR Sir, – Having this day sold the last copy of the first edition (of x thousand) of the 'Kickleburys Abroad,' and having orders for more, had we not better proceed to a second edition? and will you permit me to enclose an order on,”

Singular coincidence! And if every author who was so abused by a critic had a similar note from a publisher, good Lord! how easily would we take the critic's censure!

“Yes, yes,” you say; “it is all very well for a writer to affect to be indifferent to a critique from the Times. You bear it as a boy bears a flogging at school, without crying out; but don't swagger and brag as if you liked it."

Let us have truth before all. I would rather have a good word than a bad one from any person: but if a critic abuses me from a high place, and it is worth my while, I will appeal. If I can show that the judge who is delivering sentence against me, and laying down the law and making a pretence of learning, has no learning and no law, and is neither more nor less than a pompous noodle, who ought not to be heard in any respectable court, I will do so; and then, dear friends, perhaps you will have something to laugh at in this book.–

"THE KICKLEBURYS ABROAD.

"It has been customary, of late years, for the purveyors of amusing literature – the popular authors of the day – to put forth certain opuscules, denominated 'Christmas Books,' with the ostensible intention of swelling the tide of exhilaration, or other expansive emotions, incident upon the exodus of the old and the inauguration of the new year. We have said that their ostensible intention was such, because there is another motive for these productions, locked up (as the popular author deems) in his own breast, but which betrays itself, in the quality of the work, as his principal incentive. Oh! that any muse should be set upon a high stool to cast up accounts and balance a ledger! Yet so it is; and the popular author finds it convenient to fill up the declared deficit, and place himself in a position the more effectually to encounter those liabilities which sternly assert themselves contemporaneously and in contrast with the careless and freehanded tendencies of the season by the emission of Christmas books – a kind of literary assignats, representing to the emitter expunged debts, to the receiver an investment of enigmatical value. For the most part bearing the stamp of their origin in the vacuity of the writer's exchequer rather than in the fulness of his genius, they suggest by their feeble flavor the rinsings of a void brain after the more important concoctions of the expired year. Indeed, we should as little think of taking these compositions as examples of the merits of their authors as we should think of measuring the valuable services of Mr. Walker, the postman, or Mr. Bell, the dust-collector, by the copy of verses they leave at our doors as a provocative of the expected annual gratuity – effusions with which they may fairly be classed for their intrinsic worth no less than their ultimate purport.

"In the Christmas book presently under notice, the author appears (under the thin disguise of Mr. Michael Angelo Titmarsh) in 'propria persona' as the popular author, the contributor to Punch, the remorseless pursuer of unconscious vulgarity and feeblemindedness, launched upon a tour of relaxation to the Rhine. But though exercising, as is the wont of popular authors in their moments of leisure, a plentiful reserve of those higher qualities to which they are indebted for their fame, his professional instincts are not altogether in abeyance. From the moment his eye lights upon a luckless family group embarked on the same steamer with himself, the sight of his accustomed quarry – vulgarity, imbecility, and affectation – reanimates his relaxed sinews, and, playfully fastening his satiric fangs upon the familiar prey, he dallies with it in mimic ferocity like a satiated mouser.

"Though faintly and carelessly indicated, the characters are those with which the author loves to surround himself. A tuft-hunting county baronet's widow, an inane captain of dragoons, a graceless young baronet, a lady with groundless pretensions to feeble health and poesy, an obsequious nonentity her husband, and a flimsy and artificial young lady, are the personages in whom we are expected to find amusement. Two individuals alone form an exception to the above category, and are offered to the respectful admiration of the reader, – the one, a shadowy serjeant-at-law, Mr. Titmarsh's travelling companion, who escapes with a few side puffs of flattery, which the author struggles not to render ironical, and a mysterious countess, spoken of in a tone of religious reverence, and apparently introduced that we may learn by what delicate discriminations our adoration of rank should be regulated.

"To those who love to hug themselves in a sense of superiority by admeasurement with the most worthless of their species, in their most worthless aspects, the Kickleburys on the Rhine will afford an agreeable treat, especially as the purveyor of the feast offers his own moments of human weakness as a modest entree in this banquet of erring mortality. To our own, perhaps unphilo-sophical, taste the aspirations towards sentimental perfection of another popu-lar author are infinitely preferable to these sardonic divings after the pearl of truth, whose lustre is eclipsed in the display of the diseased oyster. Much, in the present instance, perhaps all, the disagreeable effect of his subject is no doubt attributable to the absence of Mr. Thackeray's usual brilliancy of style. A few flashes, however, occur, such as the description of M. Lenoir's gaming establishment, with the momentous crisis to which it was subjected, and the quaint and imaginative sallies evoked by the whole town of Rougetnoirbourg and its lawful prince. These, with the illustrations, which are spirited enough, redeem the book from an absolute ban. Mr. Thackeray's pencil is more congenial than his pen. He cannot draw his men and women with their skins off, and, therefore, the effigies of his characters are pleasanter to contemplate than the flayed anatomies of the letterpress."

There is the whole article. And the reader will see (in the paragraph preceding that memorable one which winds up with the diseased oyster) that he must be a worthless creature for daring to like the book, as he could only do so from a desire to hug himself in a sense of superiority by admeasurement with the most worthless of his fellow-creatures!

The reader is worthless for liking a book of which all the characters are worthless, except two, which are offered to his respectful admiration; and of these two the author does not respect one, but struggles not to laugh in his face; whilst he apparently speaks of another in a tone of religious reverence, because the lady is a countess, and because he (the author) is a sneak. So reader, author, characters, are rogues all. Be there any honest men left, Hal? About Printing-house Square, mayhap you may light on an honest man, a squeamish man, a proper moral man, a man that shall talk you Latin by the half-column if you will but hear him.

And what a style it is, that great man's! What hoighth of foine language entoirely! How he can discoorse you in English for all the world as if it was Latin! For instance, suppose you and I had to announce the important news that some writers published what are called Christmas books; that Christmas books are so called because they are published at Christmas: and that the purpose of the authors is to try and amuse people. Suppose, I say, we had, by the sheer force of intellect, or by other means of observation or information, discovered these great truths, we should have announced them in so many words. And there it is that the difference lies between a great writer and a poor one; and we may see how an inferior man may fling a chance away. How does my friend of the Times put these propositions? "It has been customary," says he, "of late years for the purveyors of amusing literature to put forth certain opuscules, denominated Christmas books, with the ostensible intention of swelling the tide of exhilaration, or other expansive emotions, incident upon the exodus of the old or the inauguration of the new year." That is something like a sentence; not a word scarcely but's in Latin, and the longest and handsomest out of the whole dictionary. That is proper economy – as you see a buck from Holywell Street put every pinchbeck pin, ring, and chain which he possesses about his shirt, hands, and waistcoat, and then go and cut a dash in the Park, or swagger with his order to the theatre. It costs him no more to wear all his ornaments about his distinguished person than to leave them at home. If you can be a swell at a cheap rate, why not? And I protest, for my part, I had no idea what I was really about in writing and submitting my little book for sale, until my friend the critic, looking at the article, and examining it with the eyes of a connoisseur, pronounced that what I had fancied simply to be a book was in fact "an opuscule denominated so-and-so, and ostensibly intended to swell the tide of expansive emotion incident upon the inauguration of the new year." I can hardly believe as much even now – so little do we know what we really are after, until men of genius come and interpret.

And besides the ostensible intention, the reader will perceive that my judge has discovered another latent motive, which I had "locked up in my own breast." The sly rogue! (if we may so speak of the court.) There is no keeping anything from him; and this truth, like the rest, has come out, and is all over England by this time. Oh, that all England, which has bought the judge's charge, would purchase the prisoner's plea in mitigation! "Oh, that any muse should be set on a high stool," says the bench, "to cast up accounts and balance a ledger! Yet so it is; and the popular author finds it convenient to fill up the declared deficit by the emission of Christmas books – a kind of assignats that bear the stamp of their origin in the vacuity of the writer's exchequer." There is a trope for you! You rascal, you wrote because you wanted money! His lordship has found out what you were at, and that there is a deficit in your till. But he goes on to say that we poor devils are to be pitied in our necessity; and that these compositions are no more to be taken as examples of our merits than the verses which the dustman leaves at his lordship's door, "as a provocative of the expected annual gratuity," are to be considered as measuring his, the scavenger's, valuable services – nevertheless the author's and the scavenger's "effusions may fairly be classed, for their intrinsic worth, no less than their ultimate purport."

Heaven bless his lordship on the bench – What a gentle manlike badinage he has, and what a charming and playful wit always at hand! What a sense he has for a simile, or what Mrs. Malaprop calls an odorous comparison, and how gracefully he conducts it to "its ultimate purport." A gentleman writing a poor little book is a scavenger asking for a Christmas-box!

As I try this small beer which has called down such a deal of thunder, I can't help thinking that it is not Jove who has interfered (the case was scarce worthy of his divine vindictiveness); but the Thunderer's man, Jupiter Jeames, taking his master's place, adopting his manner, and trying to dazzle and roar like his awful employer. That figure of the dustman has hardly been flung from heaven: that "ultimate purport" is a subject which the Immortal would hardly handle. Well, well; let us allow that the book is not worthy of such a polite critic – that the beer is not strong enough for a gentleman who has taste and experience in beer.

That opinion no man can ask his honor to alter; but (the beer being the question), why make unpleasant allusions to the Gazette, and hint at the probable bankruptcy of the brewer? Why twit me with my poverty; and what can the Times' critic know about the vacuity of my exchequer? Did he ever lend me any money? Does he not himself write for money? (and who would grudge it to such a polite and generous and learned author?) If he finds no disgrace in being paid, why should I? If he has ever been poor, why should he joke at my empty exchequer? Of course such a genius is paid for his work: with such neat logic, such a pure style, such a charming poetical turn of phrase, of course a critic gets money. Why, a man who can say of a Christmas book that "it is an opuscule denominated so-and-so, and ostensibly intended to swell the tide of expansive emotion incident upon the exodus of the old year," must evidently have had immense sums and care expended on his early education, and deserves a splendid return. You can't go into the market, and get scholarship like THAT, without paying for it: even the flogging that such a writer must have had in early youth (if he was at a public school where the rods were paid for), must have cost his parents a good sum. Where would you find any but an accomplished classical scholar to compare the books of the present (or indeed any other) writer to "sardonic divings after the pearl of truth, whose lustre is eclipsed in the display of the diseased oyster;" mere Billingsgate doesn't turn out oysters like these; they are of the Lucrine lake:– this satirist has pickled his rods in Latin brine. Fancy, not merely a diver, but a sardonic diver: and the expression of his confounded countenance on discovering not only a pearl, but an eclipsed pearl, which was in a diseased oyster! I say it is only by an uncommon and happy combination of taste, genius, and industry, that a man can arrive at uttering such sentiments in such fine language, – that such a man ought to be well paid, as I have no doubt he is, and that he is worthily employed to write literary articles, in large type, in the leading journal of Europe. Don't we want men of eminence and polite learning to sit on the literary bench, and to direct the public opinion?

But when this profound scholar compares me to a scavenger who leaves a copy of verses at his door and begs for a Christmas-box, I must again cry out and say, "My dear sir, it is true your simile is offensive, but can you make it out? Are you not hasty in your figures and illusions?" If I might give a hint to so consummate a rhetorician, you should be more careful in making your figures figures, and your similes like: for instance, when you talk of a book "swelling the tide of exhilaration incident to the inauguration of the new year," or of a book "bearing the stamp of its origin in vacuity," of a man diving sardonically; or of a pearl eclipsed in the display of a diseased oyster – there are some people who will not apprehend your meaning: some will doubt whether you had a meaning: some even will question your great powers, and say, "Is this man to be a critic in a newspaper, which knows what English, and Latin too, and what sense and scholarship, are?" I don't quarrel with you – I take for granted your wit and learning, your modesty and benevolence – but why scavenger – Jupiter Jeames – why scavenger? A gentleman, whose biography the Examiner was fond of quoting before it took its present serious and orthodox turn, was pursued by an outraged wife to the very last stage of his existence with an appeal almost as pathetic – Ah, sir, why scavenger?

How can I be like a dustman that rings for a Christmas-box at your hall-door? I never was there in my life. I never left at your door a copy of verses provocative of an annual gratuity, as your noble honor styles it. Who are you? If you are the man I take you to be, it must have been you who asked the publisher for my book, and not I who sent it in, and begged a gratuity of your worship. You abused me out of the Times' window; but if ever your noble honor sent me a gratuity out of your own door, may I never drive another dustcart. "Provocative of a gratuity!" O splendid swell! How much was it your worship sent out to me by the footman? Every farthing you have paid I will restore to your lordship, and I swear I shall not be a halfpenny the poorer.

As before, and on similar seasons and occasions, I have compared myself to a person following a not dissimilar calling: let me suppose now, for a minute, that I am a writer of a Christmas farce, who sits in the pit, and sees the performance of his own piece. There comes applause, hissing, yawning, laughter, as may be: but the loudest critic of all is our friend the cheap buck, who sits yonder and makes his remarks, so that all the audience may hear. "THIS a farce!" says Beau Tibbs: "demmy! it's the work of a poor devil who writes for money, – confound his vulgarity! This a farce! Why isn't it a tragedy, or a comedy, or an epic poem, stap my vitals? This a farce indeed! It's a feller as sends round his 'at, and appeals to charity. Let's 'ave our money back again, I say." And he swaggers off; – and you find the fellow came with an author's order.

But if, in spite of Tibbs, our "kyind friends," the little farce, which was meant to amuse Christmas (or what my classical friend calls Exodus), is asked for, even up to Twelfth Night, – shall the publisher stop because Tibbs is dissatisfied? Whenever that capitalist calls to get his money back, he may see the letter from the respected publisher, informing the author that all the copies are sold, and that there are demands for a new edition. Up with the curtain, then! Vivat Regina! and no money returned, except the Times "gratuity!"

M. A. TITMARSH.

January 5, 1851.

THE KICKLEBURYS ON THE RHINE.

The cabman, when he brought us to the wharf, and made his usual charge of six times his legal fare, before the settlement of which he pretended to refuse the privilege of an exeat regno to our luggage, glared like a disappointed fiend when Lankin, calling up the faithful Hutchison, his clerk, who was in attendance, said to him, "Hutchison, you will pay this man. My name is Serjeant Lankin, my chambers are in Pump Court. My clerk will settle with you, sir." The cabman trembled; we stepped on board; our lightsome luggage was speedily whisked away by the crew; our berths had been secured by the previous agency of

Hutchison; and a couple of tickets, on which were written, "Mr. Serjeant Lankin," "Mr. Titmarsh," (Lankin's, by the way, incomparably the best and comfortablest sleeping place,) were pinned on to two of the curtains of the beds in a side cabin when we descended.

Who was on board? There were Jews, with Sunday papers and fruit; there were couriers and servants straggling about; there were those bearded foreign visitors of England, who always seem to decline to shave or wash themselves on the day of a voyage, and, on the eve of quitting our country, appear inclined to carry away as much as possible of its soil on their hands and linen: there were parties already cozily established on deck under the awning; and steady-going travellers for'ard, smoking already the pleasant morning cigar, and watching the phenomena of departure.

The bell rings: they leave off bawling, "Anybody else for the shore?" The last grape and Bell's Life merchant has scuffled over the plank: the Johns of the departing nobility and gentry line the brink of the quay, and touch their hats:

Hutchison touches his hat to me – to ME, heaven bless him! I turn round inexpressibly affected and delighted, and whom do I see but Captain Hicks!

"Hallo! YOU here?" says Hicks, in a tone which seems to mean, "Confound you, you are everywhere."

Hicks is one of those young men who seem to be everywhere a great deal too often.

How are they always getting leave from their regiments? If they are not wanted in this country, (as wanted they cannot be, for you see them sprawling over the railing in Rotten Row all day, and shaking their heels at every ball in town,) – if they are not wanted in this country, I say, why the deuce are they not sent off to India, or to Demerara, or to Sierra Leone, by Jove? – the farther the better; and I should wish a good unwholesome climate to try 'em, and make 'em hardy. Here is this Hicks, then – Captain Launcelot Hicks, if you please – whose life is nothing but breakfast, smoking, riding-school, billiards, mess, polking, billiards, and smoking again, and da capo – pulling down his moustaches, and going to take a tour after the immense labors of the season.

"How do you do, Captain Hicks?" I say. "Where are you going?"

"Oh, I am going to the Whine," says Hicks; "evewybody goes to the Whine." The WHINE indeed! I dare say he can no more spell properly than he can speak.

"Who is on board – anybody?" I ask, with the air of a man of fashion. "To whom does that immense pile of luggage belong – under charge of the lady's-maid, the courier, and the British footman? A large white K is painted on all the boxes."

"How the deuce should I know?" says Hicks, looking, as I fancy, both red and angry, and strutting off with his great cavalry lurch and swagger: whilst my friend the Serjeant looks at him lost in admiration, and surveys his shining little boots, his chains and breloques, his whiskers and ambrosial moustaches, his gloves and other dandifications, with a pleased wonder; as the ladies of the Sultan's harem surveyed the great Lady from Park Lane who paid them a visit; or the simple subjects of Montezuma looked at one of Cortes's heavy dragoons.

That must be a marquis at least," whispers Lankin, who consults me on points of society, and is pleased to have a great opinion of my experience.

I burst out in a scornful laugh. "THAT!" I say; "he is a captain of dragoons, and his father an attorney in Bedford Row. The whiskers of a roturier, my good Lankin, grow as long as the beard of a Plantagenet. It don't require much noble blood to learn the polka. If you were younger, Lankin, we might go for a shilling a night, and dance every evening at M. Laurent's Casino, and skip about in a little time as well as that fellow. Only we despise the kind of thing you know, – only we're too grave, and too steady."

"And too fat," whispers Lankin, with a laugh.

"Speak for yourself, you maypole," says I. "If you can't dance yourself, people can dance round you – put a wreath of flowers upon your old poll, stick you up in a village green, and so make use of you."

"I should gladly be turned into anything so pleasant," Lankin answers; "and so, at least, get a chance of seeing a pretty girl now and then. They don't show in Pump Court, or at the University Club, where I dine. You are a lucky fellow, Titmarsh, and go about in the world. As for me, I never –"

"And the judges' wives, you rogue?" I say. "Well, no man is satisfied; and the only reason I have to be angry with the captain yonder is, that, the other night, at Mrs. Perkins's, being in conversation with a charming young creature – who knows all my favorite passages in Tennyson, and takes a most delightful little line of opposition in the Church controversy – just as we were in the very closest, dearest, pleasantest part of the talk, comes up young Hotspur yonder, and whisks her away in a polka. What have you and I to do with polkas, Lankin? He took her down to supper – what have you and I to do with suppers?"

Our duty is to leave them alone," said the philosophical Serjeant. "And now about breakfast – shall we have some?" And as he spoke, a savory little procession of stewards and stewards' boys, with drab tin dish-covers, passed from the caboose, and descended the stairs to the cabin. The vessel had passed Greenwich by this time, and had worked its way out of the mast-forest which guards the approaches of our city.

The owners of those innumerable boxes, bags, oilskins, guitar-cases, whereon the letter K was engraven, appeared to be three ladies, with a slim gentleman of two or three and thirty, who was probably the husband of one of them. He had numberless shawls under his arm and guardianship. He had a strap full of Murray's Handbooks and Continental Guides in his keeping; and a little collection of parasols and umbrellas, bound together, and to be carried in state before the chief of the party, like the lictor's fasces before the consul.

The chief of the party was evidently the stout lady. One parasol being left free, she waved it about, and commanded the luggage and the menials to and fro. "Horace, we will sit there," she exclaimed, pointing to a comfortable place on the deck. Horace went and placed the shawls and the Guidebooks. "Hirsch, avy vou conty les bagages? tront sett morso ong too?" The German courier said, "Oui, miladi," and bowed a rather sulky assent. "Bowman, you will see that Finch is comfortable, and send her to me." The gigantic Bowman, a gentleman in an undress uniform, with very large and splendid armorial buttons, and with traces of the powder of the season still lingering in his hair, bows, and speeds upon my lady's errand.

I recognize Hirsch, a well-known face upon the European highroad, where he has travelled with many acquaintances. With whom is he making the tour now? – Mr. Hirsch is acting as courier to Mr. and Mrs. Horace Milliken. They have not been married many months, and they are travelling, Hirsch says, with a contraction of his bushy eyebrows, with miladi, Mrs. Milliken's mamma. "And who is her ladyship?" Hirsch's brow contracts into deeper furrows. "It is Miladi Gigglebury," he says, "Mr. Didmarsh. Berhabs you know her." He scowls round at her, as she calls out loudly, "Hirsch, Hirsch!" and obeys that summons.

It is the great Lady Kicklebury of Pocklington Square, about whom I remember Mrs. Perkins made so much ado at her last ball; and whom old Perkins conducted to supper. When Sir Thomas Kicklebury died (he was one of the first tenants of the Square), who does not remember the scutcheon with the coronet with two balls, that flamed over No. 36? Her son was at Eton then, and has subsequently taken an honorary degree at Oxford, and been an ornament of Platt's and the "Oswestry Club." He fled into St. James's from the great house in Pocklington Square, and from St. James's to Italy and the Mediterranean, where he has been for some time in a wholesome exile. Her eldest daughter's marriage with Lord Roughhead was talked about last year; but Lord Roughhead, it is known, married Miss Brent; and Horace Milliken, very much to his surprise, found himself the affianced husband of Miss Lavinia Kicklebury, after an agitating evening at Lady Polkimore's, when Miss Lavinia, feeling herself faint, went out on to the leads (the terrace, Lady Polkimore WILL call it), on the arm of Mr. Milliken. They were married in January: it's not a bad match for Miss K. Lady Kicklebury goes and stops for six months of the year at Pigeoncot with her daughter and son-in-law; and now that they are come abroad, she comes too. She must be with Lavinia, under the present circumstances.

When I am arm-in-arm, I tell this story glibly off to Lankin, who is astonished at my knowledge of the world, and says, "Why, Titmarsh, you know everything."

"I DO know a few things, Lankin my boy," is my answer. "A man don't live in society, and PRETTY GOOD society, let me tell you, for nothing."

The fact is, that all the above details are known to almost any man in our neighborhood. Lady Kicklebury does not meet with US much, and has greater folks than we can pretend to be at her parties. But we know about THEM. She'll conde-scend to come to Perkins's, WITH WHOSE FIRM SHE BANKS; and she MAY overdraw HER ACCOUNT: but of that, of course, I know nothing.

When Lankin and I go down stairs to breakfast, we find, if not the best, at least the most conspicuous places in occupation of Lady Kicklebury's party, and the hulking London footman making a darkness in the cabin, as he stoops through it bearing cups and plates to his employers.

[Why do they always put mud into coffee on board steamers? Why does the tea generally taste of boiled boots? Why is the milk scarce and thin? And why do they have those bleeding legs of boiled mutton for dinner? I ask why? In the steamers of other nations you are well fed. Is it impossible that Britannia, who confessedly rules the waves, should attend to the victuals a little, and that meat should be well cooked under a Union Jack? I just put in this question, this most interesting question, in a momentous parenthesis, and resume the tale.]

When Lankin and I descend to the cabin, then, the tables are full of gobbling people; and, though there DO seem to be a couple of places near Lady Kicklebury, immediately she sees our eyes directed to the inviting gap, she slides out, and with her ample robe covers even more than that large space to which by art and nature she is entitled, and calling out, "Horace, Horace!" and nodding, and winking, and pointing, she causes her son-in-law to extend the wing on his side. We are cut of THAT chance of a breakfast. We shall have the tea at its third water, and those two damp black muttonchops, which nobody else will take, will fall to our cold share.

At this minute a voice, clear and sweet, from a tall lady in a black veil, says, "Mr. Titmarsh," and I start and murmur an ejaculation of respectful surprise, as I recognize no less a person than the Right Honorable the Countess of Knightsbridge, taking her tea, breaking up little bits of toast with her slim fingers, and sitting between a Belgian horse-dealer and a German violoncello-player who has a conge after the opera – like any other mortal.

I whisper her ladyship's name to Lankin. The Serjeant looks towards her with curiosity and awe. Even he, in his Pump Court solitudes, has heard of that star of fashion – that admired amongst men, and even women – that Diana severe yet simple, the accomplished Aurelia of Knightsbridge. Her husband has but a small share of HER qualities. How should he? The turf and the fox-chase are his delights – the smoking-room at the "Travellers –" – nay, shall we say it? – the illuminated arcades of "Vauxhall," and the gambols of the dishevelled Terpsichore. Knightsbridge has his faults – ah! even the peerage of England is not exempt from them. With Diana for his wife, he flies the halls where she sits severe and serene, and is to be found (shrouded in smoke, 'tis true,) in those caves where the contrite chimneysweep sings his terrible death chant, or the Bacchanalian judge administers a satiric law. Lord Knightsbridge has his faults, then; but he has the gout at Rougetnoir-bourg, near the Rhine, and thither his wife is hastening to minister to him.

"I have done," says Lady Knightsbridge, with a gentle bow, as she rises; "you may have this place, Mr. Titmarsh; and I am sorry my breakfast is over: I should have prolonged it had I thought that YOU were coming to sit by me. Thank you – my glove." (Such an absurd little glove, by the way). "We shall meet on the deck when you have done."

And she moves away with an august curtsy. I can't tell how it is, or what it is, in that lady; but she says, "How do you do?" as nobody else knows how to say it. In all her actions, motions, thoughts, I would wager there is the same calm grace and harmony. She is not very handsome, being very thin, and rather sad-looking. She is not very witty, being only up to the conversation, whatever it may be; and yet, if she were in black serge, I think one could not help seeing that she was a Princess, and Serene Highness; and if she were a hundred years old, she could not be but beautiful. I saw her performing her devotions in Antwerp Cathedral, and forgot to look at anything else there;so calm and pure, such a sainted figure hers seemed.

When this great lady did the present writer the honor to shake his hand (I had the honor to teach writing and the rudiments of Latin to the young and intelligent Lord Viscount Pimlico), there seemed to be a commotion in the Kicklebury party – heads were nodded together, and turned towards Lady Knightsbridge: in whose honor, when Lady Kicklebury had sufficiently reconnoitred her with her eyeglass, the baronet's lady rose and swept a reverential curtsy, backing until she fell up against the cushions at the stern of the boat. Lady Knightsbridge did not see this salute, for she did not acknowledge it, but walked away slimly (she seems to glide in and out of the room), and disappeared up the stair to the deck.

Lankin and I took our places, the horse-dealer making room for us; and I could not help looking, with a little air of triumph, over to the Kicklebury faction, as much as to say, "You fine folks, with your large footman and supercilious airs, see what WE can do."

As I looked – smiling, and nodding, and laughing at me, in a knowing, pretty way, and then leaning to mamma as if in explanation, what face should I see but that of the young lady at Mrs. Perkins's, with whom I had had that pleasant conversation which had been interrupted by the demand of Captain Hicks for a dance? So, then, that was Miss Kicklebury, about whom Miss Perkins, my young friend, has so often spoken to me: the young ladies were in conversation when I had the happiness of joining them; and Miss P. went away presently, to look to her guests) – that is Miss Fanny Kicklebury.

A sudden pang shot athwart my bosom – Lankin might have perceived it, but the honest Serjeant was so awestricken by his late interview with the Countess of Knightsbridge, that his mind was unfit to grapple with other subjects – a pang of feeling (which I concealed under the grin and graceful bow wherewith Miss Fanny's salutations were acknowledged) tore my heartstrings – as I thought of – I need not say – of HICKS.

He had danced with her, he had supped with her – he was here, on board the boat. Where was that dragoon? I looked round for him. In quite a far corner, – but so that he could command the Kicklebury party, I thought, – he was eating his breakfast, the great healthy oaf, and consuming one broiled egg after another.

In the course of the afternoon, all parties, as it may be supposed, emerged upon deck again, and Miss Fanny and her mamma began walking the quarterdeck with a quick pace, like a couple of post-captains. When Miss Fanny saw me, she stopped and smiled, and recognized the gentleman who had amused her so at Mrs. Perkins's. What a dear sweet creature Eliza Perkins was! They had been at school together. She was going to write to Eliza everything that happened on the voyage.

"EVERYTHING?" I said, in my particularly sarcastic manner.

"Well, everything that was worth telling. There was a great number of things that were very stupid, and of people that were very stupid. Everything that YOU say, Mr. Titmarsh, I am sure I may put down. You have seen Mr. Titmarsh's funny books, mamma?"

Mamma said she had heard – she had no doubt they were very amusing. "Was not that – ahem – Lady Knightsbridge, to whom I saw you speaking, sir?"

"Yes; she is going to nurse Lord Knightsbridge, who has the gout at Rougetnoirbourg."

"Indeed! how very fortunate! what an extraordinary coincidence! We are going too," said Lady Kicklebury.

I remarked "that everybody was going to Rougetnoirbourg this year; and I heard of two gentlemen – Count Carambole and Colonel Cannon – who had been obliged to sleep there on a billiard-table for want of a bed."

"My son Kicklebury – are you acquainted with Sir Thomas Kicklebury?" her ladyship said, with great stateliness – "is at Noirbourg, and will take lodgings for us. The springs are particularly recommended for my daughter, Mrs. Milliken and, at great personal sacrifice, I am going thither myself:, but what will not a mother do, Mr. Titmarsh? Did I understand you to say that you have the – the entree at Knightsbridge House? The parties are not what they used to be, I am told. Not that I have any knowledge. I am but a poor country baronet's widow, Mr. Titmarsh; though the Kickleburys date from Henry III., and MY family is not of the most modern in the country. You have heard of General Guff, my father, perhaps? aide-de-camp to the Duke of York, and wounded by his Royal Highness's side at the bombardment of Valenciennes. WE move IN OUR OWN SPHERE."

"Mrs. Perkins is a very kind creature," I said, "and it was a very pleasant ball. Did you not think so, Miss Kicklebury?"

"I thought it odious," said Miss Fanny. "I mean, it WAS pleasant until that – that stupid man – what was his name? – came and took me away to dance with him."

"What! don't you care for a red coat and moustaches?" I asked.

"I adore genius, Mr. Titmarsh," said the young lady, with a most killing look of her beautiful blue eyes, "and I have every one of your works by heart – all, except the last, which I can't endure. I think it's wicked, positively wicked – My darling Scott – how can you? And are you going to make a Christmas-book this year?"

"Shall I tell you about it?"

"Oh, do tell us about it," said the lively, charming creature, clapping her hands: and we began to talk, being near Lavinia (Mrs. Milliken) and her husband, who was ceaselessly occupied in fetching and carrying books, biscuits, pillows and cloaks, scent-bottles, the Italian greyhound, and the thousand and one necessities of the pale and interesting bride. Oh, how she did fidget! how she did grumble! how she altered and twisted her position! and how she did make poor Milliken trot!

After Miss Fanny and I had talked, and I had told her my plan, which she pronounced to be delightful, she continued:– "I never was so provoked in my life, Mr. Titmarsh, as when that odious man came and interrupted that dear delightful conversation."

"On your word? The odious man is on board the boat: I see him smoking just by the funnel yonder, look! and looking at us."

"He is very stupid," said Fanny; "and all that I adore is intellect, dear Mr. Titmarsh."

"But why is he on board?" said I, with a fin sourire.

"Why is he on board? Why is everybody on board? How do we meet? (and oh, how glad I am to meet you again!) You don't suppose that I know how the horrid man came here?"

"Eh! he may be fascinated by a pair of blue eyes, Miss Fanny! Others have been so," I said.

"Don't be cruel to a poor girl, you wicked, satirical creature," she said. "I think Captain Hicks odious – there! and I was quite angry when I saw him on the boat. Mamma does not know him, and she was so angry with me for dancing with him that night: though there was nobody of any particular mark at poor dear Mrs. Perkins's – that is, except YOU, Mr. Titmarsh."

"And I am not a dancing man," I said, with a sigh.

"I hate dancing men; they can do nothing but dance."

O yes, they can. Some of them can smoke, and some can ride, and some of them can even spell very well."

"You wicked, satirical person. I'm quite afraid of you!"

"And some of them call the Rhine the 'Whine, –" I said, giving an admirable imitation of poor Hicks's drawling manner.

Fanny looked hard at me, with a peculiar expression on her face. At last she laughed. "Oh, you wicked, wicked man," she said, "what a capital mimic you are, and so full of cleverness! Do bring up Captain Hicks – isn't that his name? – and trot him out for us. Bring him up, and introduce him to mamma: do now, go!"

Mamma, in the meanwhile, had waited her time, and was just going to step down the cabin stairs as Lady Knightsbridge ascended from them. To draw back, to make a most profound curtsy, to exclaim, "Lady Knightsbridge! I have had the honor of seeing your ladyship at – hum – hum – hum" (this word I could not catch) – "House," – all these feats were performed by Lady Kicklebury in one instant, and acknowledged with the usual calmness by the younger lady.

"And may I hope," continues Lady Kicklebury, "that that most beautiful of all children – a mother may say so – that Lord Pimlico has recovered his hooping-cough? We were so anxious about him. Our medical attendant is Mr. Topham, and he used to come from Knightsbridge House to Pocklington Square, often and often. I am interested about the hooping-cough. My own dear boy had it most severely; that dear girl, my eldest daughter, whom you see stretched on the bench – she is in a very delicate state, and only lately married – not such a match as I could have wished: but Mr. Milliken is of a good family, distantly related to your ladyship's. A Milliken, in George the Third's reign, married a Boltimore, and the Boltimores, I think, are your first-cousins. They married this year, and Lavinia is so fond of me, that she can't part with me, and I have come abroad just to please her. We are going to Noirbourg. I think I heard from my son that Lord Knightsbridge was at Noirbourg."

"I believe I have had the pleasure of seeing Sir Thomas Kicklebury at Knightsbridge House," Lady Knightsbridge said, with something of sadness.

"Indeed!" and Kicklebury had never told her! He laughed at her when she talked about great people: he told her all sorts of ridiculous stories when upon this theme. But, at any rate, the acquaintance was made: Lady Kicklebury would not leave Lady Knightsbridge; and, even in the throes of seasickness, and the secret recesses of the cabin, WOULD talk to her about the world, Lord Pimlico, and her father, General Guff, late aide-de-camp to the Duke of York.

That those throes of sickness ensued, I need not say. A short time after passing Ramsgate, Serjeant Lankin, who had been exceedingly gay and satirical – (in his calm way; he quotes Horace, my favorite bits as an author, to myself, and has a quiet snigger, and, so to speak, amontillado flavor, exceedingly pleasant)

– Lankin, with a rueful and livid countenance, descended into his berth, in the which that six foot of serjeant packed himself I don't know how.

When Lady Knightsbridge went down, down went Kicklebury. Milliken and his wife stayed, and were ill together on deck. A palm of glory ought to be awarded to that man for his angelic patience, energy, and suffering. It was he who went for Mrs. Milliken's maid, who wouldn't come to her mistress; it was he, the shyest of men, who stormed the ladies' cabin – that maritime harem – in order to get her mother's bottle of salts; it was he who went for the brandy-and-water, and begged, and prayed, and besought his adored Lavinia to taste a leetle drop. Lavinia's reply was, "Don't – go away – dont tease, Horace," and so forth. And, when not wanted, the gentle creature subsided on the bench, by his wife's feet, and was sick in silence.

[Mem – In married life, it seems to me, that it is almost always Milliken and wife, or just the contrary. The angels minister to the tyrants; or the gentle, henpecked husband cowers before the superior partlet. if ever I marry, I know the sort of woman I will choose; and I won't try her temper by overindulgence, and destroy her fine qualities by a ruinous subserviency to her wishes.]

Little Miss Fanny stayed on deck, as well as her sister, and looked at the stars of heaven, as they began to shine there, and at the Foreland lights as we passed them. I would have talked with her; I would have suggested images of poesy, and thoughts of beauty; I would have whispered the word of sentiment – the delicate allusion – the breathing of the soul that longs to find a congenial heart – the sorrows and aspirations of the wounded spirit, stricken and sad, yet not QUITE despairing; still knowing that the hope-plant lurked in its crushed ruins – still able to gaze on the stars and the ocean, and love their blazing sheen, their boundless azure. I would, I say, have taken the opportunity of that stilly night to lay bare to her the treasures of a heart that, I am happy to say, is young still; but circumstances forbade the frank outpouring of my poet soul: in a word, I was obliged to go and lie down on the flat of my back, and endeavor to control

OTHER emotions which struggled in my breast.

Once, in the night-watches, I arose, and came on deck; the vessel was not, methought, pitching much; and yet – and yet Neptune was inexorable. The placid stars looked down, but they gave me no peace. Lavinia Milliken seemed asleep, and her Horace, in a deathlike torpor, was huddled at her feet. Miss Fanny had quitted the larboard side of the ship, and had gone to starboard; and I thought that there was a gentleman beside her; but I could not see very clearly, and returned to the horrid crib, where Lankin was asleep, and the German fiddler underneath him was snoring like his own violoncello.

In the morning we were all as brisk as bees. We were in the smooth waters of the lazy Scheldt. The stewards began preparing breakfast with that matutinal eagerness which they always show. The sleepers in the cabin were roused from their horsehair couches by the stewards' boys nudging, and pushing, and flapping tablecloths over them. I shaved and made a neat toilette, and came upon deck just as we lay off that little Dutch fort, which is, I dare say, described in "Murray's guidebook," and about which I had some rare banter with poor Hicks and Lady Kicklebury, whose sense of humor is certainly not very keen. He had, somehow, joined her ladyship's party, and they were looking at the fort, and its tri-colored flag – that floats familiar in Vandevelde's pictures – and at the lazy shipping, and the tall roofs, and dumpy church towers, and flat pastures, lying before us in a Cuyplike haze.

I am sorry to say, I told them the most awful fibs about that fort. How it had been defended by the Dutch patriot, Van Swammerdam, against the united forces of the Duke of Alva and Marshal Turenne, whose leg was shot off as he was leading the last unsuccessful assault, and who turned round to his aide-de-camp and said, Allez dire an Premier Consul, que je meurs avec regret de ne pas avoir assez fait pour la France!" which gave Lady Kicklebury an opportunity to placer her story of the Duke of York, and the bombardment of Valenciennes; and caused young Hicks to look at me in a puzzled and appealing manner and hint that I was "chaffing."

"Chaffing indeed!" says I, with a particularly arch eye-twinkle at Miss Fanny. "I wouldn't make fun of you, Captain Hicks! If you doubt my historical accuracy, look at the 'Biographie Universelle.' I say – look at the 'Biographie Universelle. –"

He said, "O– ah – the 'Biogwaphie Universelle' may be all vewy well, and that; but I never can make out whether you are joking or not, somehow; and I always fancy you are going to CAWICK-ACHAW me. Ha, ha!" And he laughed, the good-natured dragoon laughed, and fancied he had made a joke.

I entreated him not to be so severe upon me; and again he said, "Haw haw!" and told me, "I mustn't expect to have it all MY OWN WAY, and if I gave a hit, I must expect a Punch in return. Haw haw!" Oh, you honest young Hicks!

Everybody, indeed, was in high spirits. The fog cleared off, the sun shone, the ladies chatted and laughed, even Mrs.

Milliken was in good humor ("My wife is all intellect," Milliken says, looking at her with admiration), and talked with us freely and gayly. She was kind enough to say that it was a great pleasure to meet with a literary and well-informed person – that one often lived with people that did not comprehend one. She asked if my companion, that tall gentleman – Mr. Serjeant Lankin, was he? – was literary. And when I said that Lankin knew more Greek, and more Latin, and more law, and more history, and more everything, than all the passengers put together, she vouchsafed to look at him with interest, and enter into a conversation with my modest friend the Serjeant. Then it was that her adoring husband said "his Lavinia was all intellect;" – Lady Kicklebury saying that SHE was not a literary woman: that in HER day few acquirements were requisite for the British female; but that she knew THE SPIRIT OF THE AGE, and her DUTY AS A MOTHER, and that "Lavinia and Fanny had had the best masters and the best education which money and constant maternal solicitude could impart." If our matrons are virtuous, as they are, and it is Britain's boast, permit me to say that they certainly know it.

The conversation growing powerfully intellectual under Mrs. Milliken, poor Hicks naturally became uneasy, and put an end to literature by admiring the ladies' headdresses. "Cab-heads, hoods, what do you call 'em?" he asked of Miss Kicklebury. Indeed, she and her sister wore a couple of those blue silk over-bonnets, which have lately become the fashion, and which I never should have mentioned but for the young lady's reply.

"Those hoods!" she said — "WE CALL THOSE HOODS UGLIES! Captain Hicks."

Oh, how pretty she looked as she said it! The blue eyes looked up under the blue hood, so archly and gayly; ever so many dimples began playing about her face; her little voice rang so fresh and sweet, that a heart which has never loved a tree or flower but the vegetable in question was sure to perish — a heart worn down and sickened by repeated disappointment, mockery, faithlessness — a heart whereof despair is an accustomed tenant, and in whose desolate and lonely depths dwells an abiding gloom, began to throb once more – began to beckon Hope from the window – began to admit sunshine – began to – O Folly, Folly! O Fanny! O Miss K., how lovely you looked as you said, "We call those hoods Uglies!" Ugly indeed!

This is a chronicle of feelings and characters, not of events and places, so much. All this time our vessel was making rapid way up the river, and we saw before us the slim towers of the noble cathedral of Antwerp soaring in the rosy sunshine. Lankin and I had agreed to go to the "Grand Laboureur," or the Place de Meir. They give you a particular kind of jam-tarts there – called Nun's tarts, I think – that I remember, these twenty years, as the very best tarts – as good as the tarts which we ate when we were boys. The "Laboureur" is a dear old quiet comfortable hotel; and there is no man in England who likes a good dinner better than Lankin.

"What hotel do you go to?" I asked of Lady Kicklebury.

"We go to the 'Saint Antoine' of course. Everybody goes to the 'Saint Antoine, –" her ladyship said. "We propose to rest here; to do the Rubens's; and to proceed to Cologne tomorrow. Horace, call Finch and Bowman; and your courier, if he will have the condescension to wait upon ME, will perhaps look to the baggage."

"I think, Lankin," said I, "as everybody seems going to the 'Saint Antoine,' we may as well go, and not spoil the party."

"I think I'll go too," says Hicks; as if HE belonged to the party.

And oh, it was a great sight when we landed, and at every place at which we paused afterwards, to see Hirsch over the Kicklebury baggage, and hear his polyglot maledictions at the porters! If a man sometimes feels sad and lonely at his bachelor condition, if SOME feelings of envy pervade his heart, at seeing beauty on another's arm, and kind eyes directed towards a happier mug than his own – at least there are some consolations in travelling, when a fellow has but one little portmanteau or bag which he can easily shoulder, and thinks of the innumerable bags and trunks which the married man and the father drags after him. The married Briton on a tour is but a luggage overseer: his luggage is his morning thought, and his nightly terror. When he floats along the Rhine he has one eye on a ruin, and the other on his luggage. When he is in the railroad he is always thinking, or ordered by his wife to think, "is the luggage safe?" It clings round him. It never leaves him (except when it DOES leave him, as a trunk or two will, and make him doubly miserable). His carpetbags lie on his chest at night, and his wife's forgotten bandbox haunts his turbid dreams.

I think it was after she found that Lady Kicklebury proposed to go to the "Grand Saint Antoine" that Lady Knightsbridge put herself with her maid into a carriage and went to the other inn. We saw her at the cathedral, where she kept aloof from our party. Milliken went up the tower, and so did Miss Fanny. I am too old a traveller to mount up those immeasurable stairs, for the purpose of making myself dizzy by gazing upon a vast map of low countries stretched beneath me, and waited with Mrs. Milliken and her mother below.

When the tower-climbers descended, we asked Miss Fanny and her brother what they had seen.

"We saw Captain Hicks up there," remarked Milliken. "And I am very glad you didn't come, Lavinia my love. The excitement would have been too much for you, quite too much."

All this while Lady Kicklebury was looking at Fanny, and Fanny was holding her eyes down; and I knew that between her and this poor Hicks there could be nothing serious, for she had laughed at him and mimicked him to me half a dozen times in the course of the day.

We "do the Rubens's," as Lady Kicklebury says; we trudge from cathedral to picture-gallery, from church to church. We see the calm old city, with its towers and gables, the bourse, and the vast town-hall; and I have the honor to give Lady Kicklebury my arm during these peregrinations, and to hear a hundred particulars regarding her ladyship's life and family. How Milliken has been recently building at Pigeoncot; how he will have two thousand a year more when his uncle dies; how she had peremptorily to put a stop to the assiduities of that unprincipled young man, Lord Roughhead, whom Lavinia always detested, and who married Miss Brent out of sheer pique. It was a great escape for her darling Lavinia. Roughhead is a most wild and dissipated young man, one of Kicklebury's Christchurch friends, of whom her son has too many, alas! and she enters into many particulars respecting the conduct of Kicklebury – the unhappy boy's smoking, his love of billiards, his fondness for the turf: she fears he has already injured his income, she fears he is even now playing at Noirbourg; she is going thither to wean him, if possible, from his companions and his gayeties – what may not a mother effect? She only wrote to him the day before they left London to announce that she was marching on him with her family. He is in many respects like his poor father – the same openness and frankness, the same easy disposition: alas! the same love of pleasure. But she had reformed the father, and will do her utmost to call back her dear misguided boy. She had an advantageous match for him in view – a lady not beautiful in person, it is true, but possessed of every good principle, and a very, very handsome fortune. It was under pretence of flying from this lady that Kicklebury left town. But she knew better.

I say young men will be young men, and sow their wild oats; and think to myself that the invasion of his mamma will be perhaps more surprising than pleasant to young Sir Thomas Kicklebury, and that she possibly talks about herself and her family, and her virtues and her daughters, a little too much: but she WILL make a confidant of me, and all the time we are doing the Rubens's she is talking of the pictures at Kicklebury, of her portrait by Lawrence, pronounced to be his finest work, of Lavinia's talent for drawing, and the expense of Fanny's music-masters; of her house in town (where she hopes to see me); of her parties which were stopped by the illness of her butler. She talks Kicklebury until I am sick. And oh, Miss Fanny, all of this I endure, like an old fool, for an occasional sight of your bright eyes and rosy face!

[Another parenthesis. – "We hope to see you in town, Mr. Titmarsh." Foolish mockery! If all the people whom one has met abroad, and who have said, "We hope to meet you often in town," had but made any the slightest efforts to realize their hopes by sending a simple line of invitation through the penny post, what an enormous dinner acquaintance one would have had! But I mistrust people who say, "We hope to see you in town."]

Lankin comes in at the end of the day, just before dinnertime. He has paced the whole town by himself – church, tower, and fortifications, and Rubens, and all. He is full of Egmont and Alva. He is up to all the history of the siege, when Chassee defended, and the French attacked the place. After dinner we stroll along the quays; and over the quiet cigar in the hotel court, Monsieur Lankin discourses about the Rubens pictures, in a way which shows that the learned Serjeant has an eye for pictorial beauty as well as other beauties in this world, and can rightly admire the vast energy, the prodigal genius, the royal splendor of the King of Antwerp. In the most modest way in the world he has remarked a student making clever sketches at the Museum, and has ordered a couple of copies from him of the famous Vandyke and the wondrous adoration of the Magi, "a greater picture," says he, "than even the cathedral picture; in which opinion those may agree who like." He says he thinks Miss Kicklebury is a pretty little thing; that all my swans are geese; and that as for that old woman, with her airs and graces, she is the most intolerable old nuisance in the world. There is much good judgment, but there is too much sardonic humor about Lankin. He cannot appreciate women properly. He is spoiled by being an old bachelor, and living in that dingy old Pump Court; where, by the way, he has a cellar fit for a Pontiff. We go to rest; they have given us humble lodgings high up in the building, which we accept like philosophers who travel with but a portmanteau apiece. The Kickleburys have the grand suite, as becomes their dignity. Which, which of those twinkling lights illumines the chamber of Miss Fanny?

Hicks is sitting in the court too, smoking his cigar. He and Lankin met in the fortifications. Lankin says he is a sensible fellow, and seems to know his profession. "Every man can talk well about something," the Serjeant says. "And one man can about everything," says I; at which Lankin blushes; and we take our flaring tallow candles and go to bed. He has us up an hour before the starting time, and we have that period to admire Herr Oberkellner, who swaggers as becomes the Oberkellner of a house frequented by ambassadors; who contradicts us to our faces, and whose own countenance is ornamented with yesterday's beard, of which, or of any part of his clothing, the graceful youth does not appear to have divested himself since last we left him. We recognize, somewhat dingy and faded, the elaborate shirtfront which appeared at yesterday's banquet. Farewell, Herr Oberkellner! May we never see your handsome countenance, washed or unwashed, shaven or unshorn, again!

"Here come the ladies: "Good morning, Miss Fanny." I hope you slept well, Lady Kicklebury?" "A tremendous bill?" "No wonder; how can you expect otherwise, when you have such a bad dinner?" Hearken to Hirsch's comminations over the luggage! Look at the honest Belgian soldiers, and that fat Freyschutz on guard, his rifle in one hand, and the other hand in his pocket. Captain Hicks bursts into a laugh at the sight of the fat Freyschutz, and says, "By Jove, Titmarsh, you must cawickachaw him." And we take our seats at length and at leisure, and the railway trumpets blow, and (save for a brief halt) we never stop till night, trumpeting by green flats and pastures, by broad canals and old towns, through Liege and Verviers, through Aix and Cologne, till we are landed at Bonn at nightfall.

We all have supper, or tea – we have become pretty intimate – we look at the strangers' book, as a matter of course, in the great room of the "Star Hotel." Why, everybody is on the Rhine! Here are the names of half one's acquaintance.

"I see Lord and Lady Exborough are gone on," says Lady Kicklebury, whose eye fastens naturally on her kindred aristocracy. "Lord and Lady Wyebridge and suite, Lady Zedland and her family."

"Hallo! here's Cutler of the Onety-oneth, and MacMull of the Greens, en route to Noirbourg," says Hicks, confidentially. "Know MacMull? Devilish good fellow — such a fellow to smoke."

Lankin, too, reads and grins. "Why, are they going the Rhenish circuit?" he says, and reads:

Sir Thomas Minos, Lady Minos, nebst Begleitung, aus England.

Sir John AEacus, mit Familie und Dienerschaft, aus England.

Sir Roger Raadamanthus.

Thomas Smith, Serjeant.

Serjeant Brown and Mrs. Brown, aus England.

Serjeant Tomkins, Anglais. Madame Tomkins, Mesdemoiselles Tomkins.

Monsieur Kewsy, Conseiller de S. M. la Reine d'Angleterre. Mrs. Kewsy, three Miss Kewsys.

And to this list Lankin, laughing, had put down his own name, and that of the reader's obedient servant, under the august autograph of Lady Kicklebury, who signed for herself, her son-in-law, and her suite.

Yes, we all flock the one after the other, we faithful English folks. We can buy Harvey Sauce, and Cayenne Pepper, and Morison's Pills, in every city in the world. We carry our nation everywhere with us; and are in our island, wherever we go. Toto divisos orbe — always separated from the people in the midst of whom we are.

When we came to the steamer next morning, "the castled crag of Drachenfels" rose up in the sunrise before, and looked as pink as the cheeks of Master Jacky, when they have been just washed in the morning. How that rosy light, too, did become Miss Fanny's pretty dimples, to be sure! How good a cigar is at the early dawn! I maintain that it has a flavor which it does not possess at later hours, and that it partakes of the freshness of all Nature. And wine, too: wine is never so good as at breakfast; only one can't drink it, for tipsiness's sake.

See! there is a young fellow drinking soda-water and brandy already. He puts down his glass with a gasp of satisfaction. It is evident that he had need of that fortifier and refresher. He puts down the beaker and says, "How are you, Titmarsh? I was SO cut last night. My eyes, wasn't I! Not in the least: that's all."

It is the youthful descendant and heir of an ancient line: the noble Earl of Grimsby's son, Viscount Talboys. He is travelling with the Rev. Baring Leader, his tutor; who, having a great natural turn and liking towards the aristocracy, and having inspected Lady Kicklebury's cards on her trunks, has introduced himself to her ladyship already, and has inquired after Sir Thomas Kicklebury, whom he remembers perfectly, and whom he had often the happiness of meeting when Sir Thomas was an undergraduate at Oxford. There are few characters more amiable, and delightful to watch and contemplate, than some of those middle-aged Oxford bucks who hang about the university and live with the young tufts. Leader can talk racing and boating with the fastest young Christchurch gentleman. Leader occasionally rides to cover with Lord Talboys; is a good shot, and seldom walks out without a setter or a spaniel at his heels. Leader knows the "Peerage" and the "Racing Calendar" as well as the Oxford cram-books. Leader comes up to town and dines with Lord Grimsby. Leader goes to Court every two years. He is the greatest swell in his common-room. He drinks claret, and can't stand port-wine any longer; and the old fellows of his college admire him, and pet him, and get all their knowledge of the world and the aristocracy from him. I admire those kind old dons when they appear affable and jaunty, men of the world, members of the "Camford and Oxbridge Club," upon the London pavement. I like to see them over the Morning Post in the common-room; with a "Ha, I see Lady Rackstraw has another daughter." "Poppleton there has been at another party at X— House, and YOU weren't asked, my boy." – "Lord Coverdale has got a large party staying at Coverdale. Did you know him at Christchurch? He was a very handsome man before he broke his nose fighting the bargeman at Iffly: a light weight, but a beautiful sparrer," Let me add that Leader, although he does love a tuft, has a kind heart: as his mother and sisters in Yorkshire know; as all the village knows too – which is proud of his position in the great world, and welcomes him very kindly when he comes down and takes the duty at Christmas, and preaches to them one or two of "the very sermons which Lord Grimsby was good enough to like, when I delivered them at Talboys."

"You are not acquainted with Lord Talboys?" Leader asks, with a degage air. "I shall have much pleasure in introducing you to him. Talboys, let me introduce you to Lady Kicklebury. Sir Thomas Kicklebury was not at Christchurch in your time; but you have heard of him, I dare say. Your son has left a reputation at Oxford."

"I should think I have, too. He walked a hundred miles in a hundred hours. They said he bet that he'd drink a hundred pints of beer in a hundred hours: but I don't think he could do it – not strong beer; don't think any man could. The beer here isn't worth a –"

"My dear Talboys," says Leader, with a winning smile, "I suppose Lady Kicklebury is not a judge of beer – and what an unromantic subject of conversation here, under the castled crag immortalized by Byron."

"What the deuce does it mean about peasant-girls with dark blue eyes, and hands that offer corn and wine?" asks Talboys. "I'VE never seen any peasant-girls, except the – ugliest set of women I ever looked at."

"The poet's license. I see, Miliken, you are making a charming sketch. You used to draw when you were at Brasenose, Milliken; and play – yes, you played the violoncello."

Mr. Milliken still possessed these accomplishments. He was taken up that very evening by a soldier at Coblentz, for making a sketch of Ehrenbreitstein. Mrs. Milliken sketches immensely too, and writes poetry: such dreary pictures, such dreary poems! but professional people are proverbially jealous; and I doubt whether our fellow-passenger, the

German, would even allow that Milliken could play the violoncello.

Lady Kicklebury gives Miss Fanny a nudge when Lord Talboys appears, and orders her to exert all her fascinations. How the old lady coaxes, and she wheedles! She pours out the Talboys' pedigree upon him; and asks after his aunt, and his mother's family. Is he going to Noirbourg? How delightful! There is nothing like British spirits; and to see an English matron well set upon a young man of large fortune and high rank, is a great and curious sight.

And yet, somehow, the British dogged-ness does not always answer. "Do you know that old woman in the drab jacket, Titmarsh?" my hereditary legislator asks of me. "What the devil is she bothering ME for, about my aunts, and setting her daughter at me? I ain't such a fool as that. I ain't clever, Titmarsh; I never said I was. I never pretend to be clever, and that – but why does that old fool bother ME, hay? Heigho! I'm devilish thirsty. I was devilish cut last night. I think I must have another go-off. Hallo you! Kellner! Garsong! Ody soda, Oter petty vare do dyvee de Conac. That's your sort; isn't it, Leader?"

"You will speak French well enough, if you practise," says Leader with a tender voice; "practice is everything. Shall we dine at the table-d'hote? Waiter! put down the name of Viscount Talboys and Mr. Leader, if you please."

The boat is full of all sorts and conditions of men. For'ard, there are peasants and soldiers: stumpy, placid-looking little warriors for the most part, smoking feeble cigars and looking quite harmless under their enormous helmets. A poor stunted dull-looking boy of sixteen, staggering before a black-striped sentry-box, with an enormous musket on his shoulder, does not seem to me a martial or awe-inspiring object. Has it not been said that we carry our prejudices everywhere, and only admire what we are accustomed to admire in our own country?

Yonder walks a handsome young soldier who has just been marrying a wife. How happy they seem! and how pleased that everybody should remark their happiness.

It is a fact that in the full sunshine, and before a couple of hundred people on board the Joseph Miller steamer, the soldier absolutely kissed Mrs. Soldier; at which the sweet Fanny Kicklebury was made to blush.

We were standing together looking at the various groups: the pretty peasant-woman (really pretty for once,) with the red headdress and fluttering ribbons, and the child in her arms; the jolly fat old gentleman, who was drinking Rhine-wine before noon, and turning his back upon all the castles, towers, and ruins, which reflected their crumbling peaks in the water; upon the handsome young students who came with us from Bonn, with their national colors in their caps, with their picturesque looks, their yellow ringlets, their budding moustaches, and with cuts upon almost every one of their noses, obtained in duels at the university: most picturesque are these young fellows, indeed – but ah, why need they have such black hands?

Near us is a type, too: a man who adorns his own tale, and points his own moral.

"Yonder, in his carriage, sits the Count de Reineck, who won't travel without that dismal old chariot, though it is shabby, costly, and clumsy, and though the wicked red republicans come and smoke under his very nose. Yes, Miss Fanny, it is the lusty young Germany, pulling the nose of the worn-out old world."

"Law, what DO you mean, Mr. Titmarsh?" cries the dear Fanny.

"And here comes Mademoiselle de Reineck, with her companion. You see she is wearing out one of the faded silk gowns which she has spoiled at the Residenz during the season: for the Reinecks are economical, though they are proud; and forced, like many other insolvent grandees, to do and to wear shabby things.

"It is very kind of the young countess to call her companion 'Louise,' and to let Louise call her 'Laure;' but if faces may be trusted, – and we can read in one countenance conceit and tyranny; deceit and slyness in another, – dear Louise has to suffer some hard raps from dear Laure: and, to judge from her dress, I don't think poor Louise has her salary paid very regularly.

"What a comfort it is to live in a country where there is neither insolence nor bankruptcy among the great folks, nor cringing, nor flattery among the small. Isn't it, Miss Fanny?"

Miss Fanny says, that she can't understand whether I am joking or serious; and her mamma calls her away to look at the ruins of Wigginstein. Everybody looks at Wigginstein. You are told in Murray to look at Wigginstein.

Lankin, who has been standing by, with a grin every now and then upon his sardonic countenance, comes up and says, "Titmarsh, how can you be so impertinent?"

"Impertinent! as how?"

"The girl must understand what you mean; and you shouldn't laugh at her own mother to her. Did you ever see anything like the way in which that horrible woman is following the young lord about?"

"See! You see it every day, my dear fellow; only the trick is better done, and Lady Kicklebury is rather a clumsy practitioner. See! why nobody is better aware of the springes which are set to catch him than that young fellow himself, who is as knowing as any veteran in May Fair. And you don't suppose that Lady Kicklebury fancies that she is doing anything mean, or anything wrong? Heaven bless you! she never did anything wrong in her life. She has no idea but that everything she says, and thinks, and does is right. And no doubt she never did rob a church: and was a faithful wife to Sir Thomas, and pays her tradesmen. Confound her virtue! It is that which makes her so wonderful — that brass armor in which she walks impenetrable — not knowing what pity is, or charity; crying sometimes when she is vexed, or thwarted, but laughing never; cringing, and domineering by the same natural instinct — never doubting about herself above all. Let us rise, and revolt against those people, Lankin. Let us war with them, and smite them utterly. It is to use against these, especially, that Scorn and Satire were invented."

"And the animal you attack," says Lankin, "is provided with a hide to defend him – it is a common ordinance of nature."

And so we pass by tower and town, and float up the Rhine. We don't describe the river. Who does not know it? How you see people asleep in the cabins at the most picturesque parts, and angry to be awakened when they fire off those stupid guns for the echoes! It is as familiar to numbers of people as Greenwich; and we know the merits of the inns along the road as if they were the "Trafalgar" or the "Star and Garter." How stale everything grows! If we were to live in a garden of Eden, now, and the gate were open, we should go out, and tramp forward, and push on, and get up early in the morning, and push on again – anything to keep moving, anything to get a change: anything but quiet for the restless children of Cain.

So many thousands of English folks have been at Rougetnoirbourg in this and last seasons, that it is scarcely needful to alter the name of that pretty little gay, wicked place. There were so many British barristers there this year that they called the "Hotel des Quatre Saisons" the "Hotel of Quarter Sessions." There were judges and their wives, serjeants and their ladies, Queen's counsel learned in the law, the Northern circuit and the Western circuit: there were officers of half-pay and full-pay, military officers, naval officers, and sheriffs' officers. There were people of high fashion and rank, and people of no rank at all; there were men and women of reputation, and of the two kinds of reputation; there were English boys playing cricket; English pointers putting up the German partridges, and English guns knocking them down; there were women whose husbands, and men whose wives were at home; there were High Church and Low Church – England turned out for a holiday, in a word. How much farther shall we extend our holiday ground, and where shall we camp next? A winter at Cairo is nothing now. Perhaps ere long we shall be going to Saratoga Springs, and the Americans coming to Margate for the summer.

Apartments befitting her dignity and the number of her family had been secured for Lady Kicklebury by her dutiful son, in the same house in which one of Lankin's friends had secured for us much humbler lodgings. Kicklebury received his mother's advent with a great deal of good humor; and a wonderful figure the good-natured little baronet was when he presented himself to his astonished friends, scarcely recognizable by his own parent and sisters, and the staring retainers of their house.

"Mercy, Kicklebury! have you become a red republican?" his mother asked.

"I can't find a place to kiss you," said Miss Fanny, laughing to her brother; and he gave her pretty cheek such a scrub with his red beard, as made some folks think it would be very pleasant to be Miss Fanny's brother.

In the course of his travels, one of Sir Thomas Kicklebury's chief amusements and cares had been to cultivate this bushy auburn ornament. He said that no man could pronounce German properly without a beard to his jaws; but he did not appear to have got much beyond this preliminary step to learning; and, in spite of his beard, his honest English accent came out, as his jolly English face looked forth from behind that fierce and bristly decoration, perfectly good-humored and unmistakable. We try our best to look like foreigners, but we can't. Every Italian mendicant or Pont Neuf beggar knows his Englishman in spite of blouse, and beard, and slouched hat. "There is a peculiar highbred grace about us," I whisper to Lady Kicklebury, "an aristocratic je ne scais quoi, which is not to be found in any but Englishmen; and it is that which makes us so immensely liked and admired all over the Continent." Well, this may be truth or joke – this may be a sneer or a simple assertion: our vulgarities and our insolences may, perhaps, make us as remarkable as that high breeding which we assume to possess. It may be that the Continental society ridicules and detests us, as we walk domineering over Europe; but, after all, which of us would denationalize himself? who wouldn't be an Englishman? Come, sir, cosmopolite as you are, passing all your winters at Rome or at Paris; exiled by choice, or poverty, from your own country; preferring easier manners, cheaper pleasures, a simpler life: are you not still proud of your British citizenship? and would you like to be a Frenchman?

Kicklebury has a great acquaintance at Noirbourg, and as he walks into the great concert-room at night, introducing his mother and sisters there, he seemed to look about with a little anxiety, lest all of his acquaintance should recognize him. There are some in that most strange and motley company with whom he had rather not exchange salutations, under present circumstances. Pleasure-seekers from every nation in the world are here, sharpers of both sexes, wearers of the stars and cordons of every court in Europe; Russian princesses, Spanish grandees, Belgian, French, and English nobles, every degree of Briton, from the ambassador, who has his conge, to the London apprentice who has come out for his fortnight's lark. Kicklebury knows them all, and has a good-natured nod for each.

"Who is that lady with the three daughters who saluted you, Kicklebury?" asks his mother.

"That is our Ambassadress at X., ma'am. I saw her yesterday buying a penny toy for one of her little children in Frankfort Fair."

Lady Kicklebury looks towards Lady X.: she makes her excellency an undeveloped curtsy, as it were; she waves her plumed head (Lady K. is got up in great style, in a rich dejeuner toilette, perfectly regardless of expense); she salutes the ambassadress with a sweeping gesture from her chair, and backs before her as before royalty, and turns to her daughters large eyes full of meaning, and spreads out her silks in state.

"And who is that distinguished-looking man who just passed, and who gave you a reserved nod?" asks her ladyship. "Is that Lord X.?"

Kicklebury burst out laughing. "That, ma'am, is Mr. Higmore, of Conduit Street, tailor, draper, and habit-maker: and I owe him a hundred pound."

"The insolence of that sort of people is really intolerable," says Lady Kicklebury. "There MUST be some distinction of classes. They ought not to be allowed to go everywhere. And who is yonder, that lady with the two boys and the – the very high complexion?" Lady Kicklebury asks.

"That is a Russian princess: and one of those little boys, the one who is sucking a piece of barley-sugar, plays, and wins five hundred louis in a night."

"Kicklebury, you do not play? Promise your mother you do not! Swear to me at this moment you do not! Where are the horrid gambling-rooms? There, at that door where the crowd is? Of course, I shall never enter them!"

"Of course not, ma'am," says the affectionate son on duty. "And if you come to the balls here, please don't let Fanny dance with anybody, until you ask me first: you understand. Fanny, you will take care."

"Yes, Tom," says Fanny.

"What, Hicks, how are you, old fellow? How is Platts? Who would have thought of you being here? When did you come?"

"I had the pleasure of travelling with Lady Kicklebury and her daughters in the London boat to Antwerp," says Captain Hicks, making the ladies a bow. Kicklebury introduces Hicks to his mother as his most particular friend – and he whispers Fanny that "he's as good a fellow as ever lived, Hicks is." Fanny says, He seems very kind and good-natured: and – and Captain Hicks waltzes very well," says Miss Fanny with a blush, "and I hope I may have him for one of my partners."

What a Babel of tongues it is in this splendid hall with gleaming marble pillars: a ceaseless rushing whisper as if the band were playing its music by a waterfall! The British lawyers are all got together, and my friend Lankin, on his arrival, has been carried off by his brother serjeants, and becomes once more a lawyer. "Well, brother Lankin," says old Sir Thomas Minos, with his venerable kind face, "you have got your rule, I see." And they fall into talk about their law matters, as they always do, wherever they are – at a club, in a ballroom, at a dinner-table, at the top of Chimborazo. Some of the young barristers appear as bucks with uncommon splendor, and dance and hang about the ladies. But they have not the easy languid deuce-may-care air of the young bucks of the Hicks and Kicklebury school – they can't put on their clothes with that happy negligence; their neck-cloths sit quite differently on them, somehow: they become very hot when they dance, and yet do not spin round near so quickly as those London youths, who have acquired experience in corpore vili, and learned to dance easily by the practice of a thousand casinos.

Above the Babel tongues and the clang of the music, as you listen in the great saloon, you hear from a neighboring room a certain sharp ringing clatter, and a hard clear voice cries out, "Zero rouge," or "Trente-cinq noir. Impair et passe." And then there is a pause of a couple of minutes, and then the voice says, "Faites le jeu, Messieurs. Le jeu est fait, rien ne va plus" – and the sharp ringing clatter recommences. You know what that room is? That is Hades. That is where the spirited proprietor of the establishment takes his toll, and thither the people go who pay the money which supports the spirited proprietor of this fine palace and gardens. Let us enter Hades, and see what is going on there.

Hades is not an unpleasant place. Most of the people look rather cheerful. You don't see any frantic gamblers gnashing their teeth or dashing down their last stakes. The winners have the most anxious faces; or the poor shabby fellows who have got systems, and are pricking down the alternations of red and black on cards, and don't seem to be playing at all. On fete days the country people come in, men and women, to gamble; and THEY seem to be excited as they put down their hard-earned florins with trembling rough hands, and watch the turn of the wheel. But what you call the good company is very quiet and easy. A man loses his mass of gold, and gets up and walks off, without any particular mark of despair. The only gentleman whom I saw at Noirbourg who seemed really affected was a certain Count de Mustacheff, a Russian of enormous wealth, who clenched his fists, beat his breast, cursed his stars, and absolutely cried with grief: not for losing money, but for neglecting to win and play upon a coup de vingt, a series in which the red was turned up twenty times running: which series, had he but played, it is clear that he might have broken M. Lenoir's bank, and shut up the gambling-house, and doubled his own fortune – when he would have been no happier, and all the balls and music, all the newspaper-rooms and parks, all the feasting and pleasure of this delightful Rougetnoirbourg would have been at an end.

For though he is a wicked gambling prince, Lenoir, he is beloved in all these regions; his establishment gives life to the town, to the lodging-house and hotelkeepers, to the milliners and hackney-coachmen, to the letters of horseflesh, to the huntsmen and gardes-de-chasse; to all these honest fiddlers and trumpeters who play so delectably. Were Lenoir's bank to break, the whole little city would shut up; and all the Noirbourgers wish him prosperity, and benefit by his good fortune.

Three years since the Noirbourgers underwent a mighty panic. There came, at a time when the chief Lenoir was at Paris, and the reins of government were in the hands of his younger brother, a company of adventurers from Belgium, with a capital of three hundred thousand francs, and an infallible system for playing rouge et noir, and they boldly challenged the bank of Lenoir, and sat down before his croupiers, and defied him. They called themselves in their pride the Contrebanque de Noirbourg: they had their croupiers and punters, even as Lenoir had his: they had their rouleaux of Napoleons, stamped with their Contrebanquish seal:– and they began to play.

As when two mighty giants step out of a host and engage, the armies stand still in expectation, and the puny privates and commonalty remain quiet to witness the combat of the tremendous champions of the war: so it is said that when the Contrebanque arrived, and ranged itself before the officers of Lenoir – rouleau to rouleau, banknote to banknote, war for war, controlment for controlment – all the minor punters and gamblers ceased their peddling play, and looked on in silence, round the verdant plain where the great combat was to be decided.

Not used to the vast operations of war, like his elder brother, Lenoir junior, the lieutenant, telegraphed to his absent chief the news of the mighty enemy who had come down upon him, asked for instructions, and in the meanwhile met the foe-man like a man. The Contre-banque of Noirbourg gallantly opened its campaign.

The Lenoir bank was defeated day after day, in numerous savage encounters. The tactics of the Contrebanquist generals were irresistible: their infernal system bore down everything before it, and they marched onwards terrible and victorious as the Macedonian phalanx. Tuesday, a loss of eighteen thousand florins; Wednesday, a loss of twelve thousand florins; Thursday, a loss of forty thousand florins: night after night, the young Lenoir had to chronicle these disasters in melancholy despatches to his chief. What was to be done? Night after night, the Noirbourgers retired home doubtful and disconsolate; the horrid Contreban-quists gathered up their spoils and retired to a victorious supper. How was it to end?

Far away at Paris, the elder Lenoir answered these appeals of his brother by sending reinforcements of money. Chests of gold arrived for the bank. The Prince of Noirbourg bade his beleaguered lieutenant not to lose heart: he himself never for a moment blenched in this trying hour of danger.

The Contrebanquists still went on victorious. Rouleau after rouleau fell into their possession. At last the news came: The Emperor has joined the Grand Army. Lenoir himself had arrived from Paris, and was once more among his children, his people. The daily combats continued: and still, still, though Napoleon was with the Eagles, the abominable Contreban-quists fought and conquered. And far greater than Napoleon, as great as Ney himself under disaster, the bold Lenoir never lost courage, never lost good-humor, was affable, was gentle, was careful of his subjects' pleasures and comforts, and met an adverse fortune with a dauntless smile.

With a devilish forbearance and coolness, the atrocious Contrebanque – like Polyphemus, who only took one of his prisoners out of the cave at a time, and so ate them off at leisure – the horrid Contrebanquists, I say, contented themselves with winning so much before dinner, and so much before supper – say five thousand florins for each meal. They played and won at noon: they played and won at eventide. They of Noirbourg went home sadly every night: the invader was carrying all before him. What must have been the feelings of the great Lenoir? What were those of Washington before Trenton, when it seemed all up with the cause of American Independence; what those of the virgin Elizabeth, when the Armada was signalled; what those of Miltiades, when the multitudinous Persian bore down on Marathon? The people looked on at the combat, and saw their chieftain stricken, bleeding, fallen, fighting still.

At last there came one day when the Contrebanquists had won their allotted sum, and were about to leave the tables which they had swept so often. But pride and lust of gold had seized upon the heart of one of their vainglorious chieftains; and he said, "Do not let us go yet – let us win a thousand florins more!" So they stayed and set the bank yet a thousand florins. The Noirbourgers looked on, and trembled for their prince.

Some three hours afterwards – a shout, a mighty shout was heard around the windows of that palace: the town, the gardens, the hills, the fountains took up and echoed the jubilant acclaim. Hip, hip, hip, hurrah, hurrah, hurrah! People rushed into each other's arms; men, women, and children cried and kissed each other. Croupiers, who never feel, who never tremble, who never care whether black wins or red loses, took snuff from each other's boxes, and laughed for joy; and Lenoir the dauntless, the INVINCIBLE Lenoir, wiped the drops of perspiration from his calm forehead, as he drew the enemy's last rouleau into his till. He had conquered. The Persians were beaten, horse and foot – the Armada had gone down. Since Wellington shut up his telescope at Waterloo, when the Prussians came charging on to the field, and the Guard broke and fled, there had been no such heroic endurance, such utter defeat, such signal and crowning victory. Vive Lenoir! I am a Lenoirite. I have read his newspapers, strolled in his gardens, listened to his music, and rejoice in his victory: I am glad he beat those

Contrebanquists. Dissipati sunt. The game is up with them.

The instances of this man's magnanimity are numerous, and worthy of Alexander the Great, or Harry the Fifth, or Robin Hood. Most gentle is he, and thoughtful to the poor, and merciful to the vanquished. When Jeremy Diddler, who had lost twenty pounds at his table, lay in inglorious pawn at his inn – when O'Toole could not leave Noirbourg until he had received his remittances from Ireland – the noble Lenoir paid Diddler's inn bill, advanced O'Toole money upon his well-known signature, franked both of them back to their native country again; and has never, wonderful to state, been paid from that day to this. If you will go play at his table, you may; but nobody forces you. If you lose, pay with a cheerful heart. Dulce est desipere in loco. This is not a treatise of morals. Friar Tuck was not an exemplary ecclesiastic, nor Robin Hood a model man; but he was a jolly outlaw; and I dare say the Sheriff of Nottingham, whose money he took, rather relished his feast at Robin's green table.

And if you lose, worthy friend, as possibly you will, at Lenoir's pretty games, console yourself by thinking that it is much better for you in the end that you should lose, than that you should win. Let me, for my part, make a clean breast of it, and own that your humble servant did, on one occasion, win a score of Napoleons; and beginning with a sum of no less than five shillings. But until I had lost them again I was so feverish, excited, and uneasy, that I had neither delectation in reading the most exciting French novels, nor pleasure in seeing pretty landscapes, nor appetite for dinner. The moment, however, that graceless money was gone, equanimity was restored: Paul Feval and Eugene Sue began to be terrifically interesting again; and the dinners at Noirbourg, though by no means good culinary specimens, were perfectly sufficient for my easy and tranquil mind. Lankin, who played only a lawyer's rubber at whist, marked the salutary change in his friend's condition; and, for my part, I hope and pray that every honest reader of this volume who plays at M. Lenoir's table will lose every shilling of his winnings before he goes away. Where are the gamblers whom we have read of? Where are the card-players whom we can remember in our early days? At one time almost every gentleman played, and there were whist-tables in every lady's drawing-room. But trumps are going out along with numbers of old-world institutions; and, before very long, a blackleg will be as rare an animal as a knight in armor.

There was a little dwarfish, abortive, counter bank set up at Noirbourg this year: but the gentlemen soon disagreed among themselves; and, let us hope, were cut off in detail by the great Lenoir. And there was a Frenchman at our inn who had won two Napoleons per day for the last six weeks, and who had an infallible system, whereof he kindly offered to communicate the secret for the consideration of a hundred louis; but there came one fatal night when the poor Frenchman's system could not make head against fortune, and her wheel went over him, and he disappeared utterly.

With the early morning everybody rises and makes his or her appearance at the Springs, where they partake of water with a wonderful energy and perseverance. They say that people get to be fond of this water at last; as to what tastes cannot men accustom themselves? I drank a couple of glasses of an abominable sort of feeble salts in a state of very gentle effervescence; but, though there was a very pretty girl who served it, the drink was abominable, and it was a marvel to see the various topers, who tossed off glass after glass, which the fair-haired little Hebe delivered sparkling from the well.

Seeing my wry faces, old Captain Carver expostulated, with a jolly twinkle of his eye, as he absorbed the contents of a sparkling crystal beaker. "Pooh! take another glass, sir: you'll like it better and better every day. It refreshes you, sir: it fortifies you: and as for liking it – gad! I remember the time when I didn't like claret. Times are altered now, ha! ha! Mrs. Fantail, madam, I wish you a very good morning. How is Fantail? He don't come to drink the water: so much the worse for him."

To see Mrs. Fantail of an evening is to behold a magnificent sight. She ought to be shown in a room by herself; and, indeed, would occupy a moderate-sized one with her person and adornments. Marie Antoinette's hoop is not bigger than Mrs. Fantail's flounces. Twenty men taking hands (and, indeed, she likes to have at least that number about her) would scarcely encompass her. Her chestnut ringlets spread out in a halo round her face: she must want two or three coiffeurs to arrange that prodigious headdress; and then, when it is done, how can she endure that extraordinary gown? Her travelling bandboxes must be as large as omnibuses.

But see Mrs. Fantail in the morning, having taken in all sail: the chestnut curls have disappeared, and two limp bands of brown hair border her lean, sallow face; you see before you an ascetic, a nun, a woman worn by mortifications, of a sad yellow aspect, drinking salts at the well: a vision quite different from that rapturous one of the previous night's ballroom. No wonder Fantail does not come out of a morning; he had rather not see such a Rebecca at the well.

Lady Kicklebury came for some mornings pretty regularly, and was very civil to Mr. Leader, and made Miss Fanny drink when his lordship took a cup, and asked Lord Talboys and his tutor to dinner. But the tutor came, and, blushing, brought an excuse from Talboys; and poor Milliken had not a very pleasant evening after Mr. Baring Leader rose to go away.

But though the water was not good the sun was bright, the music cheery, the landscape fresh and pleasant, and it was always amusing to see the vast varieties of our human species that congregated at the Springs, and trudged up and down the green allees. One of the gambling conspirators of the roulette-table it was good to see here, in his private character, drinking down pints of salts like any other sinner, having a homely wife on his arm, and between them a poodle on which they lavished their tenderest affection. You see these people care for other things besides trumps; and are not always thinking about black and red:– as even ogres are represented, in their histories, as of cruel natures, and licentious appetites, and, to be sure, fond of eating men and women; but yet it appears that their wives often respected them, and they had a sincere liking for their own hideous children. And, besides the card-players, there are band-players: every now and then a fiddle from the neighboring orchestra, or a disorganized bassoon, will step down and drink a glass of the water, and jump back into his rank again.

Then come the burly troops of English, the honest lawyers, merchants, and gentlemen, with their wives and buxom daughters, and stout sons, that, almost grown to the height of manhood, are boys still, with rough wide-awake hats and shooting-jackets, full of lark and laughter. A French boy of sixteen has had des passions ere that time, very likely, and is already particular in his dress, an ogler of the women, and preparing to kill. Adolphe says to Alphonse – "La voila cette charmante Miss Fanni, la belle Kickleburi! je te donne ma parole, elle est fraiche comme une rose! la crois-tu riche, Alphonse?" "Je me range, mon ami, vois-tu? La vie de garcon me pese. Ma parole d'honneur! je me range."

And he gives Miss Fanny a killing bow, and a glance which seems to say, "Sweet Anglaise, I know that I have won your heart."

Then besides the young French buck, whom we will willingly suppose harmless, you see specimens of the French raff, who goes aux eaux: gambler, speculator, sentimentalist, duellist, travelling with madame his wife, at whom other raffs nod and wink familiarly. This rogue is much more picturesque and civilized than the similar person in our own country: whose manners betray the stable; who never reads anything but Bell's Life; and who is much more at ease in conversing with a groom than with his employer. Here come Mr. Boucher and Mr. Fowler: better to gamble for a score of nights with honest Monsieur Lenoir, than to sit down in private once with those gentlemen. But we have said that their profession is going down, and the number of Greeks daily diminishes. They are travelling with Mr. Bloundell, who was a gentleman once, and still retains about him some faint odor of that time of bloom; and

Bloundell has put himself on young Lord Talboys, and is trying to get some money out of that young nobleman. But the English youth of the present day is a wide-awake youth, and male or female artifices are expended pretty much in vain on our young travelling companion.

Who come yonder? Those two fellows whom we met at the table-d'hote at the "Hotel de Russie" the other day: gentlemen of splendid costume, and yet questionable appearances, the eldest of whom called for the list of wines, and cried out loud enough for all the company to hear, "Lafite, six florins. 'Arry, shall we have some Lafite? You don't mind? No more do I then. I say, waiter, let's 'ave a pint of ordinaire." Truth is stranger than fiction. You good fellow, wherever you are, why did you ask 'Arry to 'ave that pint of ordinaire in the presence of your obedient servant? How could he do otherwise than chronicle the speech?

And see: here is a lady who is doubly desirous to be put into print, who encourages it and invites it. It appears that on Lankin's first arrival at Noirbourg with his travelling companion, a certain sensation was created in the little society by the rumor that an emissary of the famous Mr. Punch had arrived in the place; and, as we were smoking the cigar of peace on the lawn after dinner, looking on at the benevolent, pretty scene, Mrs. Hopkins, Miss Hopkins, and the excellent head of the family, walked many times up and down before us; eyed us severely face to face, and then walking away, shot back fierce glances at us in the Parthian manner; and at length, at the third or fourth turn, and when we could not but overhear so fine a voice, Mrs. Hopkins looks at us steadily, and says, "I'm sure he may put ME in if he likes: I don't mind."

Oh, ma'am! Oh, Mrs. Hopkins! how should a gentleman, who had never seen your face or heard of you before, want to put YOU in? What interest can the British public have in you? But as you wish it, and court publicity, here you are. Good luck go with you, madam. I have forgotten your real name, and should not know you again if I saw you. But why could not you leave a man to take his coffee and smoke his pipe in quiet?

We could never have time to make a catalogue of all the portraits that figure in this motley gallery. Among the travellers in Europe, who are daily multiplying in numbers and increasing in splendor, the United States' dandies must not be omitted. They seem as rich as the Milor of old days; they crowd in European capitals; they have elbowed out people of the old country from many hotels which we used to frequent; they adopt the French fashion of dressing rather than ours, and they grow handsomer beards than English beards: as some plants are found to flourish and shoot up prodigiously when introduced into a new soil. The ladies seem to be as well dressed as Parisians, and as handsome; though somewhat more delicate, perhaps, than the native English roses. They drive the finest carriages, they keep the grandest houses, they frequent the grandest company – and, in a word, the Broadway Swell has now taken his station and asserted his dignity amongst the grandees of Europe. He is fond of asking Count Reineck to dinner, and Grafinn Laura will condescend to look kindly upon a gentleman who has millions of dollars. Here comes a pair of New Yorkers. Behold their elegant curling beards, their velvet coats, their delicate primrose gloves and cambric handker-chiefs, and the aristocratic beauty of their boots. Why, if you had sixteen quarterings, you could not have smaller feet than those; and if you were descended from a line of kings you could not smoke better or bigger cigars.

Lady Kicklebury deigns to think very well of these young men, since she has seen them in the company of grandees and heard how rich they are. "Who is that very stylish-looking woman, to whom Mr. Washington Walker spoke just now?" she asks of Kicklebury.

Kicklebury gives a twinkle of his eye. "Oh, that, mother! that is Madame La Princesse de Mogador – it's a French title."

"She danced last night, and danced exceedingly well; I remarked her. There's a very highbred grace about the princess."

"Yes, exceedingly. We'd better come on," says Kicklebury, blushing rather as he returns the princess's nod.

It is wonderful how large Kicklebury's acquaintance is. He has a word and a joke, in the best German he can muster, for everybody – for the high wellborn lady, as for the German peasant maiden, or the pretty little washerwoman, who comes full sail down the streets, a basket on her head and one of Mrs. Fantail's wonderful gowns swelling on each arm. As we were going to the Schloss-Garten I caught a sight of the rogue's grinning face yesterday, close at little Gretel's ear under her basket; but spying out his mother advancing, he dashed down a bystreet, and when we came up with her, Gretel was alone.

One but seldom sees the English and the holiday visitors in the ancient parts of Noirbourg; they keep to the streets of new buildings and garden villas, which have sprung up under the magic influence of M. Lenoir, under the white towers and gables of the old German town. The Prince of Trente et Quarante has quite overcome the old serene sovereign of

Noirbourg, whom one cannot help fancy-
ing a prince like a prince in a Christmas
pantomime – a burlesque prince with
twopence-halfpenny for a revenue, jolly
and irascible, a prime-minister-kicking
prince, fed upon fabulous plum-puddings
and enormous pasteboard joints, by cooks
and valets with large heads which never
alter their grin. Not that this portrait is
from the life. Perhaps he has no life.
Perhaps there is no prince in the great
white tower, that we see for miles before
we enter the little town. Perhaps he has
been mediatized, and sold his kingdom
to Monsieur Lenoir. Before the palace of
Lenoir there is a grove of orange-trees in
tubs, which Lenoir bought from another
German prince; who went straightway and
lost the money, which he had been paid
for his wonderful orange-trees, over
Lenoir's green tables, at his roulette and
trente-et-quarante. A great prince is
Lenoir in his way; a generous and magnan-
imous prince. You may come to his feast
and pay nothing, unless you please. You
may walk in his gardens, sit in his palace,
and read his thousand newspapers. You
may go and play at whist in his small
drawing-rooms, or dance and hear con-
certs in his grand saloon – and there is

not a penny to pay. His fiddlers and trumpeters begin trumpeting and fiddling for you at the early dawn – they twang and blow for you in the afternoon, they pipe for you at night that you may dance – and there is nothing to pay – Lenoir pays for all. Give him but the chances of the table, and he will do all this and more. It is better to live under Prince Lenoir than a fabulous old German Durchlaucht whose cavalry ride wicker horses with petticoats, and whose prime minister has a great pasteboard head. Vive le Prince Lenoir!

There is a grotesque old carved gate to the palace of the Durchlaucht, from which you could expect none but a pantomime procession to pass. The place looks asleep; the courts are grass-grown and deserted. Is the Sleeping Beauty lying yonder, in the great white tower? What is the little army about? It seems a sham army: a sort of grotesque military. The only charge of infantry was this: one day when passing through the old town, looking for sketches. Perhaps they become croupiers at night. What can such a fabulous prince want with anything but a sham army? My favorite walk was in the ancient quarter of the town – the dear old fabulous quarter, away from the noisy actualities of life and Prince Lenoir's new palace – out of eye and earshot of the dandies and the ladies in their grand best clothes at the promenades – and the rattling whirl of the roulette wheel – and I liked to wander in the glum old gardens under the palace wall, and imagine the Sleeping Beauty within there.

Some one persuaded us one day to break the charm, and see the interior of the palace. I am sorry we did. There was no Sleeping Beauty in any chamber that we saw; nor any fairies, good or malevolent. There was a shabby set of clean old rooms, which looked as if they had belonged to a prince hard put to it for money, and whose tin crown jewels would not fetch more than King Stephen's pantaloons. A fugitive prince, a brave prince struggling with the storms of fate, a prince in exile may be poor; but a prince looking out of his own palace windows with a dressing-gown out at elbows, and dunned by his subject washerwoman – I say this is a painful object. When they get shabby they ought not to be seen.

"Don't you think so, Lady Kicklebury?" Lady Kicklebury evidently had calculated the price of the carpets and hangings, and set them justly down at a low figure. "These German princes," she said, "are not to be put on a level with English noblemen." "Indeed," we answer, "there is nothing so perfect as England: nothing so good as our aristocracy; nothing so perfect as our institutions." "Nothing! NOTHING!" says Lady K.

An English princess was once brought to reign here; and almost the whole of the little court was kept upon her dowry. The people still regard her name fondly; and they show, at the Schloss, the rooms which she inhabited. Her old books are still there – her old furniture brought from home; the presents and keepsakes sent by her family are as they were in the princess's lifetime: the very clock has the name of a Windsor maker on its face; and portraits of all her numerous race decorate the homely walls of the now empty chambers. There is the benighted old king, his beard hanging down to the star on his breast; and the first gentleman of Europe – so lavish of his portrait everywhere, and so chary of showing his royal person – all the stalwart brothers of the now all but extinct generation are there; their quarrels and their pleasures, their glories and disgraces, enemies, flatterers, detractors, admirers – all now buried. Is it not curious to think that the King of Trumps now virtually reigns in this place, and has deposed the other dynasty?

Very early one morning, wishing to have a sketch of the White Tower in which our English princess had been imprisoned, I repaired to the gardens, and set about a work, which, when completed, will no doubt have the honor of a place on the line at the Exhibition; and, returning homewards to breakfast, musing upon the strange fortunes and inhabitants of the queer, fantastic, melancholy place, behold, I came suddenly upon a couple of persons, a male and a female; the latter of whom wore a blue hood or "ugly," and blushed very much on seeing me. The man began to laugh behind his moustaches, the which cachinnation was checked by an appealing look from the young lady; and he held out his hand and said, "How d'ye do, Titmarsh? Been out making some cawickachaws, hay?"

I need not say that the youth before me was the heavy dragoon, and that the maiden was Miss Fanny Kicklebury. Or need I repeat that, in the course of my blighted being, I never loved a young gazelle to glad me with its dark blue eye, but when it came to, the usual disappointment, was sure to ensue? There is no necessity why I should allude to my feelings at this most manifest and outrageous case. I gave a withering glance of scorn at the pair, and, with a stately salutation, passed on.

Miss Fanny came tripping after me. She held out her little hand with such a pretty look of deprecation, that I could not but take it; and she said, "Mr. Titmarsh, if you please, I want to speak to you, if you please;" and, choking with emotion, I bade her speak on.

"My brother knows all about it, and, highly approves of Captain Hicks," she said, with her head hanging down; "and oh, he's very good and kind: and I know him MUCH better now, than I did when we were on board the steamer."

I thought how I had mimicked him, and what an ass I had been.

"And you know," she continued, "that you have quite deserted me for the last ten days for your great acquaintances."

"I have been to play chess with Lord Knightsbridge, who has the gout."

"And to drink tea constantly with that American lady; and you have written verses in her album; and in Lavinia's album; and as I saw that you had quite thrown me off, why I– my brother approves of it highly; and – and Captain Hicks likes you very much, and says you amuse him very much – indeed he does," says the arch little wretch. And then she added a postscript, as it were to her letter, which contained, as usual, the point which she wished to urge:–

"You – won't break it to mamma – will you be so kind? My brother will do that" – and I promised her; and she ran away, kissing her hand to me. And I did not say a word to Lady Kicklebury, and not above a thousand people at Noirbourg knew that Miss Kicklebury and Captain Hicks were engaged.

And now let those who are too confident of their virtue listen to the truthful and melancholy story which I have to relate, and humble themselves, and bear in mind that the most perfect among us are occasionally liable to fall. Kicklebury was not perfect, – I do not defend his practice. He spent a great deal more time and money than was good for him at M. Lenoir's gaming-table, and the only thing which the young fellow never lost was his good humor. If Fortune shook her swift wings and fled away from him, he laughed at the retreating pinions, and you saw him dancing and laughing as gayly after losing a rouleau, as if he was made of money, and really had the five thousand a year which his mother said was the amount of the Kicklebury property. But when her ladyship's jointure, and the young ladies' allowances, and the interest of mortgages were paid out of the five thousand a year, I grieve to say that the gallant Kicklebury's income was to be counted by hundreds and not by thousands; so that, for any young lady who wants a carriage (and who can live without one?) our friend the baronet is not a desirable specimen of bachelors. Now, whether it was that the presence of his mamma interrupted his pleasures, or certain of her ways did not please him, or that he had lost all his money at roulette and could afford no more, certain it is, that after about a fortnight's stay at Noirbourg, he went off to shoot with Count Einhorn in Westphalia; he and Hicks parting the dearest of friends, and the baronet going off on a pony which the captain lent to him. Between him and Millikin, his brother-in-law, there was not much sympathy: for he pronounced Mr. Milliken to be what is called a muff; and had never been familiar with his elder sister Lavinia, of whose poems he had a mean opinion, and who used to tease and worry him by teaching him French, and telling tales of him to his mamma, when he was a schoolboy home for the holidays. Whereas, between the baronet and Miss Fanny there seemed to be the closest affection: they walked together every morning to the waters; they joked and laughed with each other as happily as possible. Fanny was almost ready to tell fibs to screen her brother's

malpractices from her mamma: she cried
when she heard of his mishaps, and that
he had lost too much money at the green
table; and when Sir Thomas went away,
the good little soul brought him five
louis; which was all the money she had:
for you see she paid her mother
handsomely for her board; and when her
little gloves and milliner's bills were
settled how much was there left out of
two hundred a year? And she cried when
she heard that Hicks had lent Sir Thomas
money, and went up and said, "Thank
you, Captain Hicks;" and shook hands with
the captain so eagerly, that I thought he
was a lucky fellow, who had a father a
wealthy attorney in Bedford Row.
Heighho! I saw how matters were going.
The birds MUST sing in the springtime,
and the flowers bud.

Mrs. Milliken, in her character of invalid,
took the advantage of her situation to
have her husband constantly about her,
reading to her, or fetching the doctor to
her, or watching her whilst she was
dozing, and so forth; and Lady Kicklebury
found the life which this pair led rather
more monotonous than that sort of
existence which she liked, and would

leave them alone with Fanny (Captain Hicks not uncommonly coming in to take tea with the three), whilst her ladyship went to the Redoute to hear the music, or read the papers, or play a game of whist there.

The newspaper-room at Noirbourg is next to the roulette-room, into which the doors are always open; and Lady K. would come, with newspaper in hand, into this playroom, sometimes, and look on at the gamesters. I have mentioned a little Russian boy, a little imp with the most mischievous intelligence and good humor in his face, who was suffered by his parents to play as much as he chose, and who pulled bonbons out of one pocket and Napoleons out of the other, and seemed to have quite a diabolical luck at the table.

Lady Kicklebury's terror and interest at seeing this boy were extreme. She watched him and watched him, and he seemed always to win; and at last her ladyship put down just a florin – only just one florin – on one of the numbers at roulette which the little Russian imp was backing. Number twenty-seven came up, and the croupiers flung over three gold pieces and five florins to Lady Kicklebury, which she raked up with a trembling hand.

She did not play any more that night, but sat in the playroom, pretending to read the Times newspaper; but you could see her eye peering over the sheet, and always fixed on the little imp of a Russian. He had very good luck that night, and his winning made her very savage. As he retired, rolling his gold pieces into his pocket and sucking his barley-sugar, she glared after him with angry eyes; and went home, and scolded everybody, and had no sleep. I could hear her scolding. Our apartments in the Tissisch House overlooked Lady Kicklebury's suite of rooms: the great windows were open in the autumn. Yes; I could hear her scolding, and see some other people sitting whispering in the embrasure, or looking out on the harvest moon.

The next evening, Lady Kicklebury shirked away from the concert; and I saw her in the playroom again, going round and round the table; and, lying in ambush behind the Journal des Debats, I marked how, after looking stealthily round, my lady whipped a piece of money under the croupier's elbow, and (there having been no coin there previously) I saw a florin on the Zero.

She lost that, and walked away. Then she came back and put down two florins on a number, and lost again, and became very red and angry; then she retreated, and came back a third time, and a seat being vacated by a player, Lady Kicklebury sat down at the verdant board. Ah me! She had a pretty good evening, and carried off a little money again that night. The next day was Sunday: she gave two florins at the collection at church, to Fanny's surprise at mamma's liberality. On this night of course there was no play. Her ladyship wrote letters, and read a sermon.

But the next night she was back at the table; and won very plentifully, until the little Russian sprite made his appearance, when it seemed that her luck changed. She began to bet upon him, and the young Calmuck lost too. Her ladyship's temper went along with her money: first she backed the Calmuck, and then she played against him. When she played against him, his luck turned; and he began straightway to win. She put on more and more money as she lost: her winnings went: gold came out of secret pockets. She had but a florin left at last, and tried it on a number, and failed. She got up to go away. I watched her, and I watched Mr. Justice Aeacus, too, who put down a Napoleon when he thought nobody was looking.

The next day my Lady Kicklebury walked over to the moneychangers, where she changed a couple of circular notes. She was at the table that night again: and the next night, and the next night, and the next.

By about the fifth day she was like a wild woman. She scolded so, that Hirsch, the courier, said he should retire from monsieur's service, as he was not hired by Lady Kicklebury: that Bowman gave warning, and told another footman in the building that he wouldn't stand the old cat no longer, blow him if he would: that the maid (who was a Kicklebury girl) and Fanny cried: and that Mrs. Milliken's maid, Finch, complained to her mistress, who ordered her husband to remonstrate with her mother. Milliken remonstrated with his usual mildness, and, of course, was routed by her ladyship. Mrs. Milliken said, "Give me the daggers," and came to her husband's rescue. A battle royal ensued; the scared Milliken hanging about his blessed Lavinia, and entreating and imploring her to be calm. Mrs. Milliken WAS calm. She asserted her dignity as mistress of her own family: as controller of her own household, as wife of her adored husband; and she told her mamma, that with her or here she must not interfere; that she knew her duty as a child: but that she also knew it as a wife, as a – The rest of the sentence was drowned, as Milliken, rushing to her, called her his soul's angel, his adored blessing.

Lady Kicklebury remarked that Shakspeare was very right in stating how much sharper than a thankless tooth it is to have a serpent child.

Mrs. Milliken said, the conversation could not be carried on in this manner: that it was best her mamma should now know, once for all, that the way in which she assumed the command at Pigeoncot was intolerable; that all the servants had given warning, and it was with the greatest difficulty they could be soothed: and that, as their living together only led to quarrels and painful recriminations (the calling her, after her forbearance, A SERPENT CHILD, was an expression which she would hope to forgive and forget,) they had better part.

Lady Kicklebury wears a front, and, I make no doubt, a complete jasey; or she certainly would have let down her back hair at this minute, so overpowering were her feelings, and so bitter her indignation at her daughter's black ingratitude. She intimated some of her sentiments, by ejaculatory conjurations of evil. She hoped her daughter might NOT feel what ingratitude was; that SHE might never have children to turn on her and bring her to the grave with grief.

"Bring me to the grave with fiddlestick!" Mrs. Milliken said with some asperity. "And, as we are going to part, mamma, and as Horace has paid EVERYTHING on the journey as yet, and we have only brought a VERY few circular notes with us, perhaps you will have the kindness to give him your share of the travelling expenses – for you, for Fanny, and your two servants whom you WOULD bring with you: and the man has only been a perfect hindrance and great useless log, and our courier has had to do EVERY-THING. Your share is now eighty-two pounds."

Lady Kicklebury at this gave three screams, so loud that even the resolute Lavinia stopped in her speech. Her ladyship looked wildly: "Lavinia! Horace! Fanny my child," she said, "come here, and listen to your mother's shame."

"What?" cried Horace, aghast.

"I am ruined! I am a beggar! Yes; a beggar. I have lost all – all at yonder dreadful table."

"How do you mean all? How much is all?" asked Horace.

"All the money I brought with me, Horace. I intended to have paid the whole expenses of the journey: yours, this ungrateful child's – everything. But, a week ago, having seen a lovely baby's lace dress at the lace-shop; and – and – won enough at wh – wh – whoo – ist to pay for it, all but two – two florins – in an evil moment I went to the roulette-table – and lost – every shilling: and now, on may knees before you, I confess my shame."

I am not a tragic painter, and certainly won't attempt to depict THIS harrowing scene. But what could she mean by saying she wished to pay everything? She had but two twenty-pound notes: and how she was to have paid all the expenses of the tour with that small sum, I cannot conjecture.

The confession, however, had the effect of mollifying poor Milliken and his wife: after the latter had learned that her mamma had no money at all at her London bankers', and had overdrawn her account there, Lavinia consented that Horace should advance her fifty pounds upon her ladyship's solemn promise of repayment.

And now it was agreed that this highly respectable lady should return to England, quick as she might: somewhat sooner than all the rest of the public did; and leave Mr. and Mrs. Horace Milliken behind her, as the waters were still considered highly salutary to that most interesting invalid. And to England Lady Kicklebury went; taking advantage of Lord Talboys' return thither to place herself under his lordship's protection; as if the enormous Bowman was not protector sufficient for her ladyship; and as if Captain Hicks would have allowed any mortal man, any German student, any French tourist, any Prussian whiskerando, to do a harm to Miss Fanny! For though Hicks is not a brilliant or poetical genius, I am bound to say that the fellow has good sense, good manners, and a good heart; and with these qualities, a competent sum of money, and a pair of exceedingly handsome moustaches, perhaps the poor little Mrs. Launcelot Hicks may be happy.

No accident befell Lady Kicklebury on her voyage homewards: but she got one more lesson at Aix-la-Chapelle, which may serve to make her ladyship more cautious for the future: for, seeing Madame la Princesse de Mogador enter into a carriage on the railway, into which Lord Talboys followed, nothing would content Lady Kicklebury but to rush into the carriage after this noble pair; and the vehicle turned out to be what is called on the German lines, and what I wish were established in England, the Rauch Coupe. Having seated himself in this vehicle, and looked rather sulkily at my lady, Lord Talboys began to smoke: which, as the son of an English earl, heir to many thousands per annum, Lady Kicklebury permitted him to do. And she introduced herself to Madame la Princesse de Mogador, mentioning to her highness that she had the pleasure of meeting Madame la Princesse at Rougetnoirbourg; that she, Lady K., was the mother of the Chevalier de Kicklebury, who had the advantage of the acquaintance of Madame la Princesse; and that she hoped Madame la Princesse had enjoyed her stay at the waters. To these advances the Princess of Mogador returned a gracious and affable salutation, exchanging glances of peculiar meaning with two highly respectable bearded gentlemen who travelled in her suite; and, when asked by milady whereabouts her highness's residence was at Paris, said that her hotel was in the Rue Notre Dame de Lorette: where Lady Kicklebury hoped to have the honor of waiting upon Madame la Princesse de Mogador.

But when one of the bearded gentlemen called the princess by the familiar name of Fifine, and the other said, "Veux-tu fumer, Mogador?" and the princess actually took a cigar and began to smoke, Lady Kicklebury was aghast, and trembled; and presently Lord Talboys burst into a loud fit of laughter.

"What is the cause of your lordship's amusement?" asked the dowager, looking very much frightened, and blushing like a maiden of sixteen.

"Excuse me, Lady Kicklebury, but I can't help it," he said. "You've been talking to your opposite neighbor – she don't understand a word of English – and calling her princess and highness, and she's no more a princess than you or I.

She is a little milliner in the street she mentioned, and she dances at Mabille and Chateau Rouge."

Hearing these two familiar names, the princess looked hard at Lord Talboys, but he never lost countenance; and at the next station Lady Kicklebury rushed out of the smoking-carriage and returned to her own place; where, I dare say, Captain Hicks and Miss Fanny were delighted once more to have the advantage of her company and conversation. And so they went back to England, and the Kickleburys were no longer seen on the Rhine. If her ladyship is not cured of hunting after great people, it will not be for want of warning: but which of us in life has not had many warnings: and is it for lack of them that we stick to our little failings still?

When the Kickleburys were gone, that merry little Rougetnoirbourg did not seem the same place to me, somehow. The sun shone still, but the wind came down cold from the purple hills; the band played, but their tunes were stale; the promenaders paced the alleys, but I knew all their faces: as I looked out of my windows in the Tissisch house upon the great blank casements lately occupied by the Kickleburys, and remembered what a pretty face I had seen looking thence but a few days back, I cared not to look any longer; and though Mrs. Milliken did invite me to tea, and talked fine arts and poetry over the meal, both the beverage and the conversation seemed very weak and insipid to me, and I fell asleep once in my chair opposite that highly cultivated being. "Let us go back, Lankin," said I to the Serjeant, and he was nothing loth; for most of the other serjeants, barristers, and Queen's counsel were turning homewards, by this time, the period of term time summoning them all to the Temple.

So we went straight one day to Biberich on the Rhine, and found the little town full of Britons, all trooping home like ourselves. Everybody comes, and everybody goes away again, at about the same time. The Rhine innkeepers say that their customers cease with a single day almost:– that in three days they shall have ninety, eighty, a hundred guests; on the fourth, ten or eight. We do as our neighbors do. Though we don't speak to each other much when we are out a-pleasuring, we take our holiday in common, and go back to our work in gangs. Little Biberich was so full, that Lankin and I could not get rooms at the large inns frequented by other persons of fashion, and could only procure a room between us, "at the German House, where you find English comfort," says the advertisement, "with German prices."

But oh, the English comfort of those beds! How did Lankin manage in his, with his great long legs? How did I toss and tumble in mine; which, small as it was, I was not destined to enjoy alone, but to pass the night in company with anthropophagous wretched reptiles, who took their horrid meal off an English Christian! I thought the morning would never come; and when the tardy dawn at length arrived, and as I was in my first sleep, dreaming of Miss Fanny, behold I was wakened up by the Serjeant, already dressed and shaven, and who said, "Rise, Titmarsh, the steamer will be here in three-quarters of an hour." And the modest gentleman retired, and left me to dress.

The next morning we had passed by the rocks and towers, the old familiar landscapes, the gleaming towns by the riverside, and the green vineyards combed along the hills, and when I woke up, it was at a great hotel at Cologne, and it was not sunrise yet.

Deutz lay opposite, and over Deutz the dusky sky was reddened. The hills were veiled in the mist and the gray. The gray river flowed underneath us; the steamers were roosting along the quays, a light keeping watch in the cabins here and there, and its reflections quivering in the water. As I look, the skyline towards the east grows redder and redder. A long troop of gray horsemen winds down the river road, and passes over the bridge of boats. You might take them for ghosts, those gray horsemen, so shadowy do they look; but you hear the trample of their hoofs as they pass over the planks. Every minute the dawn twinkles up into the twilight; and over Deutz the heaven blushes brighter. The quays begin to fill with men: the carts begin to creak and rattle, and wake the sleeping echoes. Ding, ding, ding, the steamers' bells begin to ring: the people on board to stir and wake: the lights may be extinguished, and take their turn of sleep: the active boats shake themselves, and push out into the river: the great bridge opens, and gives them passage: the church bells of the city begin to clink: the cavalry trumpets blow from the opposite bank: the sailor is at the wheel, the porter at his burden, the soldier at his musket, and the priest at his prayers. . . .

And lo! in a flash of crimson splendor, with blazing scarlet clouds running before his chariot, and heralding his majestic approach, God's sun rises upon the world, and all nature wakens and brightens.

O glorious spectacle of light and life! O beatific symbol of Power, Love, Joy, Beauty! Let us look at thee with humble wonder, and thankfully acknowledge and adore. What gracious forethought is it – what generous and loving provision, that deigns to prepare for our eyes and to soothe our hearts with such a splendid morning festival! For these magnificent bounties of heaven to us, let us be thankful, even that we can feel thankful – (for thanks surely is the noblest effort, as it is the greatest delight, of the gentle soul) – and so, a grace for this feast, let all say who partake of it.

See! the mist clears off Drachenfels, and it looks out from the distance, and bids us a friendly farewell. Farewell to holiday and sunshine; farewell to kindly sport and pleasant leisure! Let us say good-by to the Rhine, friend. Fogs, and cares, and labor are awaiting us by the Thames; and a kind face or two looking out for us to cheer and bid us welcome.

www.ReadHowYouWant.com

You can buy our **Large Type** and **EasyRead** books from our www.ReadHowYouWant.com website, from websites like Amazon.com and through your UK and North American bookshop.

EasyRead books are designed to make your reading easy and enjoyable. **EasyRead** books are published in different font sizes, so you can select the font size best for you – **EasyRead12** is 12pt, **EasyRead14** is 14pt and so on. The **EasyRead** font, character, word and line spacing have all been set to make it as easy as possible both to recognize a word, and to run your eye along a line of text without losing your place. We split as few words as possible at line ends, as split words make reading harder and can be annoying. For out-of-copyright books, words have been changed to modern spelling (where the sense is not affected), and the original hyphenation of compound words has been retained where this improves word recognition or sense.

With most things you buy, you get a choice, and you can choose the make and model that suits best. There is a big exception – books. You don't get to choose a format that is easy for you to read – you have to read the format the publisher selects.

This "One Size Fits All" paradigm no longer need apply to books.

At www.ReadHowYouWant.com, you can order a book just as you want it, so you can read it easily. You can choose nearly any format, and at a surprisingly low cost, because of a technical breakthrough that allows us to typeset an individual book automatically, print and bind the book and have it quickly sent directly to you.

You can have your book in **Talking Book** formats **(DAISY or MP3)** or as an **E-book** or in **Braille.**

We have developed totally new visual formats which we hope will help people with **dyslexia** and other print reading disabilities. Look at www.ReadHowYouWan t.com for more information.

Good news for publishers and authors. There is a big market for large type, personalized and accessible format books. We can help publishers and authors find new market opportunities for their books, and selling your book through www.ReadH owYouWant.com is easy – we do the work for you. Contact us on info@ReadHowYouW ant.com.

Printed in the United Kingdom
by Lightning Source UK Ltd.
114939UKS00001B/133